SWAMP water was cold round her waist. The thought of snakes sent a slow, involuntary shudder through her. She dared not move. Huddled under the huge tree, she prayed the mist that had hidden her attacker would hide her too. To stand up would be to risk disaster.

Her teeth were beginning to chatter, the noise seeming unnaturally loud in the dank silence of the swamp. She clamped them together, listening. Nothing. Not a sound since the first flurry of activity, when he had come at her out of the mist, and she had ducked the weapon, hearing him (or could it have been a woman?) almost instinctively, almost in time. Instead of her temple, the blow had caught the back of her head as she turned to run, slipped on a patch of mud, and plunged into the swirling water of the Cooper River.

The river caught her like a piece of driftwood, and she had let herself go with its current, wondering, in shock and terror, whether this was the end. . . .

One Way to Venice

A NOVEL BY

Jane Aiken Hodge

FAWCETT CREST • NEW YORK

ONE WAY TO VENICE

THIS BOOK CONTAINS THE COMPLETE TEXT
OF THE ORIGINAL HARDCOVER EDITION.

Published by Fawcett Crest Books, a unit of CBS Publications,
the Consumer Publishing Division of CBS Inc.,
by arrangement with Coward, McCann & Geoghegan, Inc.

ISBN: 0-449-23466-5

Printed in the United States of America

3 4 5 6 7 8 9 10

One Way to Venice

One

THE FOURTH letter arrived on a fine, March morning, and Julia's hand shook as she tore it open. She had expected it, but not so soon. The gaps between them had been narrowing, since the first one had come in January. She did not need to refer back to them. Each message was etched hard on her brain. "He's called Dominic," the first had read, in anonymous capital letters. "Like to see him?" asked the next, mocking. "We might arrange it," said the third. And now? The words blurred for a moment before her eyes, then steadied. "Is your passport up to date?" Nothing more. The paper, standard, like that of the others. The address in capitals like the message. Fingerprints? Ridiculous. This was not the kind of thing about which one went to the police, and they, whoever they were, must know it as well as she did.

She was going to be late to the office. Never mind. She drank cold coffee without tasting it and crossed the flat's big living room to the file where she kept her papers. She knew perfectly well that her passport was good for another year, but somehow that commanding question must be obeyed. She checked. She was right. How could they know that she had checked? But in this mad world in which she found herself, anything seemed possible.

Her bus was held up in the traffic and she was very late indeed. "Sir Charles has been asking for you, Mrs. Rivers," said his secretary with just a hint of malicious pleasure. Secretaries cannot be expected to like long-established personal assistants who lunch habitually with the boss. Julia smiled a little grimly as she gathered up notebook and pen. If Miss Mitford only knew . . .

Sir Charles had known her too long and too well to be deceived by her attempt at a brisk apology. "You're in trouble again," he said, and then, aware of how she had winced at the phrase. "Sorry!"

"No need." She had known she would have to tell him sooner or later, and, now, sooner seemed best. He listened impassively, then asked the inevitable question. "You believe them?"

"Yes. I don't know why."

"You're not a fool. And it started a few months after you had given up looking for the child?"

"Yes. Which could mean anything."

"Or nothing. But of course you will have to give it a try. You've not considered the police?"

"No." In their most secret work, he and she had their own views of the police, shared with no one.

"Right, then." He summed up. "You're not well. Which is true enough, you've been looking like hell. You're going to take a holiday just as soon as I can spare you. Which will be when you get your instructions. Soon, would you think?"

"Yes. It's speeded up. I don't know how to thank you."

"Then don't try. Just come back as soon as you can. You know I can't do without you. Besides, it's my fault, in a way. I should never have let you send him for adoption in the first place. You were in no state to decide."

"Oh, God!" She swallowed a knot of tears. "If only—"

"No use," he said. "Let's get some work done. But, remember, anything I can do. . . ."

She managed a smile for him. "You've done so much already. Where in the world would I have been without you?"

"Not back in that Glasgow slum, Julia. Never think that. You'd have got away somehow, that's for sure. If I hadn't spotted that brain of yours, someone else would have. It was just my good luck that you turned up at my office door."

"And mine. I'll never be through thanking you. You've been more than a father to me."

"Nonsense." He sounded almost angry, rugged white eyebrows drawing together over the surprisingly young face. "And now, if you're going off at any moment, we'd really better get to work."

That night was full of ghosts. The old, familiar haunts of childhood: the revenants from the Glasgow slums, children no older than herself, who had lurked, hostile, on street corners, to plague her because she was different. Nameless, faceless, they had come south with her, when she had escaped at seventeen and found Sir Charles, and a career. Only in the first, incredibly happy Paris days of marriage with Breckon had she been free of them. Afterwards, she was to wonder whether they had been revenants or prophets; not memories of Glasgow, but omens for the future: the attacker in the swamp, the hand that set the torch to the guest wing. All nameless, faceless figures. But not, please God, not Breckon.

The photograph came two days later. She felt at once that the familiar envelope held something different, harder, cardboard. The boy's face was just slightly out of focus, as if the picture had been taken with a telephoto lense and very much enlarged. Water in the foreground. Black lines, on either side of the boy's head, must be bars. A railing of some kind? A prison? No—there were trees behind the bars. An orphanage? Horrible. She reached, rather blindly, for her magnifying glass and looked squarely at her child. For he *was* hers. Of that, for good or ill, there was not a shadow of doubt. He was holding on to the bars with his good left hand, the useless right one lay limp and unmistakable along the bars. Unmistakable, but also unmistakably better. Years of surgery, the doctors had said. Impossible for someone in her position. Even Sir Charles, to whom, inevitably, she had turned, had been firm to the point of ruthlessness. "For the child's sake," had been the chorus, and, suffering the double depression of childbirth and divorce, she had yielded, cried once more over the poor little helpless arm, signed the necessary papers, and collapsed.

She picked up the photograph with a shaking hand and carried it over to the window. "Dominic." It was a good name, the kind she and Breckon might have chosen. Surely, then, good people? Ridiculous. He had Breckon's high thoughtful forehead and fair hair. No telling about the eyes. No telling, either, whether he looked happy or wretched. And not much she could deduce about the blurred background, behind those sinister railings.

"Yes. Like you both." Sir Charles studied the picture carefully, then turned with distaste to the four messages. "Unpleasant people. They enjoy torturing you."

"I thought that. As if they hated me."

"Does anyone?"

"Not that I know of." Not here, at any rate, not now. What had she left for anyone to hate?

She was up early next morning, waiting for the mail. But when it came, there was no horrible, familiar envelope. Acid with disappointment, she sorted quickly through the pile of letters. A bill, a circular, an appeal for money, and—a fat manila envelope stamped "Acme Travel Agency." Another advertisement? Opened, it revealed a dark green folder, neatly labeled: *"Mrs. Rivers. One-way to Venice and hotel bookings."* And there, incredibly, it all was. A ticket, through from Victoria to Venice, by way of Basle and Milan. Reserved seats, Victoria to Folkestone, March 30, and Milan to Venice, March 31. A couchette reservation for the night. And an agency voucher for a single room, half board, at the Hotel Da Rimini, Venice, for the week beginning March 31.

And today was the twenty-eighth. Her hands shook so much that she misdialed the first time. Trying again, she got through to Acme Travel Agency at the number listed on their folder. The girl who answered was puzzled but polite. Mrs. Rivers was not happy about her bookings? But she had confirmed them herself; two days ago, when she called in, and paid cash for them.

Impossible, somehow, to ask, "What did I look like?"

"But you should have," said Sir Charles.

"I know. I'm a fool. But I'm also sure it would have got me nowhere."

"Probably. You'll go?"

"Of course."

"Well, be careful. I should miss you. And"—he held up a hand—"for God's sake don't start thanking me again."

Three days are either too long or too short a time to plan a journey. Besides, what luggage does one need to search for a child in an unknown city? She hoped, in vain, for another letter, looked up the Hotel Da Rimini and found it listed as second-class; threw some clothes into the smallest of her trousseau suitcases, and was ready two days too soon. On Sir Charles' advice, she spent them studying the large-scale map of Venice he had got for her, daunted by its maze of canal and alleyway. But surely, having led her so far, her unknown enemies—why was she so sure they were enemies?—would not abandon her now. Unless it was all some horrible, some fantastic practical joke.

If so, an expensive one, she thought, settling into her reserve seat on the three-thirty boat train from Victoria. She had arrived early on purpose, so as to be able to study her fellow travelers as they arrived. It was undeniably disconcerting to think that "they" knew exactly where she was at this moment, while she still knew nothing about them. But Sir Charles had scouted her suggestion that they might get in touch with her on the journey. If she was lucky, he thought, she would find further instructions waiting for her at the hotel. But, on their past form, they were more likely to keep her in suspense for a few days. "In which case," he had said, "go sightseeing, for God's sake. Get yourself some sunshine and a bit of colour. And learn your way round."

Her place was in a long, open carriage with tables between the seats. She had somehow expected a closed carriage for eight only, and soon gave up any serious attempt at studying the people who were now pouring on board, wandering up and down, awkward with luggage, looking for their reserved seats in the fully booked carriage. Two middle-aged women settled with sighs of relief in the aisle seats beside Julia. Their neat, small cases went easily into the rack.

"A nonsmoker, thank goodness," said one.

"Yes, but hot." From looks and voices, they were sisters. "Would you mind?" The speaker stood up and pushed open the small window beside Julia. "Just till we start?"

"Of course not." Julia was reading one of their labels, upside down, above her. The words "Brown" and "Venice" leapt out at her. It meant nothing. Half the people on the train were very likely going through to Venice.

At the far end of the carriage, a girl's voice rose, sudden and hysterical, over the general murmur. "You know I have to smoke. I bet you did it on purpose." A man's voice said something pacificatory but audible. "Second-class all the way." The angry voice rose a note higher. Heads were turning all along the carriage, but the girl, standing up and reaching an enormous leather case down from the rack, took no notice. Julia could see her now: a very expensive blonde in a fur cape. Further down the train, doors were beginning to slam. "Don't just stand there," screamed the blonde. "Can't you at least help me with this thing?"

"But honey. . . ." He kept his voice low, despite the infection of hers, and caught the heavy case just before it hit his next-door neighbour in the head. Putting it down in the aisle, he tried again. "Think of Dubrovnik in the spring." His accent was unusual. Australian, of course.

"Rain all the time." She picked up the case. "And me stuck in your pokey little pub over the marketplace, while you go out looking for 'views.' No, thanks. Little Pamela's seen the light at last." She put down the case again. "There's your bloody five-pound ring. Keep it for the next fool." Through the embarrassed British silence that had fallen on the carriage, Julia heard a whistle blow. The girl kicked her case savagely down the aisle and threw open the door at the far end of the carriage, the young man following. There was an angry shout from outside. The young man tried to hold her back as the train began to move, but she threw out the case and half fell after it.

Julia, watching, appalled, saw her trip over the case and fall spread-eagled on the platform. "My God!" The woman sitting opposite had stood up and was peering out and backwards as the train gathered speed. "I'm afraid she's really hurt herself, poor thing."

"Silly young fool," said her companion. And then, to Julia: "Do you know if that seat's taken?" No one had arrived to claim the corner seat.

"Not that I know of. Someone must have missed the train." One of "them"—the enemy? One knot, perhaps, unravelling in the web she felt around her? And yet, she wanted them to get in touch. What other hope had she of finding Dominic? And how unbearable, now that dead hope had been revived, the imagination of failure. Absorbed in gloomy thought, she hardly noticed the little bustle as the two women got themselves settled, side by side now, in the seat opposite, and started chatting happily about their plans for Venice. St. Mark's . . . the Rialto . . . time for Torcello? . . . Murano glass for Cousin Betty. . . . Julia closed her eyes, and, dreamlessly, slept.

When she woke, they were running smoothly through hopfields, ready strung for spring. The two women opposite were talking about the girl who had jumped off the train. "Might have been killed," said one.

"Or killed a porter, opening the door like that." They plunged contentedly into a well-tried discussion of the sins of the younger generation, with special reference to nephews and nieces of their own. An occasional, would-be conspiratorial glance tried to include Julia in the conversation. Did she really look so old? Twenty-eight, she thought angrily, is not exactly senility. But

then, she knew well enough that the long, lonely years
had left their mark.

The train was running past houses now; the carriage
stirred to life; in five minutes they would be in Folkestone. She pulled out the mirror Sir Charles had given
her and did a minimum, impatient job on face and
hair. Item: two eyes, brown; two lips, indifferent red.
The features that had once made her beautiful, at least
in Breckon's eyes, were all still there. It was just that
they did not, somehow, compose themselves any more.
It was years, she thought, since anyone had whistled
at her in the street.

But at least she could take care of herself. Evading
the Miss Browns, she got quickly on to the ferry, found
a chair in the bar, and a double gin and tonic. She
might be beyond wolf-whistles but she could still catch
a busy bartender's eye. Warmed by this thought, and
the gin, she went up and prowled about the deck,
almost enjoying fitful sunshine, wind in her face, and
the last views of England. If she found Dominic, there
might be some point to her life after all. Strange how
real he had become, now that he had a face and a
name. She would not imagine not finding him.

At Calais, it was raining. The drink that had cheered
now left her cold, low, and hungry. When had she
last eaten or slept properly? And, after all, this wild-
goose chase would most likely lead only to new despair,
more of it, she knew, than she could face. Well, it would
be hard on Sir Charles, but no one else would miss
her. She thought of the blond girl, risking her life
jumping off the train. Odd that in all the desperate
days since her divorce and Dominic's birth she had

never considered taking her own life. How could she? She had had a duty to Dominic, the child she had let go. But now, if she failed to find him, or—a thought that had haunted her since she saw the picture and learned his name—found him in better hands than hers. . . . Well, she still had the pills she had refused to take after her breakdown.

She walked through the green customs channel and emerged into steady drizzle to see two trains waiting on parallel tracks. Hers, the one that avoided Paris, was on the far side and her hair was wet when she got across to it. It was wetter still by the time she had established that there was no restaurant car, and, worse still, that the carriage in which her couchette was booked did not exist. The couchette attendant, shown her reservations, merely shrugged his shoulders and washed his hands of them, and her, in cockney French. It was past seven. She was hungry, she was tired, she was cold. She lost her temper and told him what she thought of him in French as fluent as and more grammatical than his own. An instinct for languages had been another of her qualifications for the job with Sir Charles.

Her French slang won her a modicum of sympathy from the attendant, but that was all. The train was fully booked. She would be lucky to find a seat for the night. As for a berth. . . . He shrugged again, abandoning her to her fate, then, as an afterthought, suggested that she might just possibly find a free berth in the wagon-lits carriage at the back of the train. But she had better hurry, he told her, maddeningly, as the train moved off.

Impossible to hurry down the crowded corridors, where some people seemed to be resigned to standing

all night, while others, more fortunate, were looking
out of windows while their berths were made up. The
refreshments trolly, with its soft drinks, sad sandwiches
and milling queue was a more serious obstacle, and by
the time she got to the wagon-lits carriage the train was
well out into darkening countryside, running fast. Here,
all was quiet, doors closed, no one in sight but the
attendant, sitting on his stool at the far end. Approached, with the most delicate hint of a bribe, he
shook his head regretfully. Here, too, everything was
fully booked. He regretted infinitely. . . .

He really did, Julia thought. The surface that Sir
Charles had made her construct for herself did have
this effect on people. She looked, and knew it, like
money, good family, and the best of taste. She felt like
death. Infuriatingly, tears began to flood down her
cheeks.

"Oh, madame." In the face of the ultimate female
weapon, the man withdrew into his cabin to consult his
papers. Emerging, "There is one possibility," he said.
"A gentleman whose companion missed the train in
London. If he could be persuaded? And if madame did
not mind sharing?"

"Good God, no," said Julia, almost as much taken
aback by her unwonted tears as he.

The attendant was already on his way down the
swaying corridor to knock on a closed door, open it,
and make his appeal in swift French.

"Quit yabbering." Julia recognised the furious voice.
"Or if you must, do it in English. You've seen my ticket,
boofhead! What's with you now?"

"There is a lady," began the attendant in halting
English, then turned, saw Julia behind him, and

switched with relief into French. "Madame, if you would explain?"

Julia had only seen the young man's back at Victoria, but the accent was unmistakable. He had to be the Australian who had been so dramatically abandoned by his girl. The compartment, with only two of its three berths made up, confirmed this. He had paid, heavily, for privacy, and was now alone with his disappointment. But at least, she congratulated herself, there was little chance that he had noticed her at the far end of the compartment at Victoria. She explained her predicament quickly, and saw the scowl deepen across what should have been a handsome, dark-browed face. He took a deep breath, and, for a moment, she steeled herself against a furious refusal. Then, lopsidedly, he smiled. "Why the hell not? All a box-up together. You don't mind. Why should I?"

"Oh, thank you!" She turned to the attendant, and found, as she had expected, that she was to pay all over again for the berth the young Australian had booked.

"He sure rooked you," said the stranger, when the man had accepted his tip, wished them a faintly salacious goodnight, and withdrawn.

"Well, of course. Frankly, I'm past caring. I can't tell you how grateful I am. My name's Julia Rivers, by the way. Mrs. Rivers."

"Tarn Menzies. 'Strine, as you've probably guessed, but no kin to the Prime Minister. Ex. You Pommies call it something funny, right? Mingies? Crazy lot." He put out a firm hand and took her case. "Shall I sling this on the rack?"

"Thanks." She had her night things in the huge, elegant shoulder bag Sir Charles had bought her.

Putting up her bag, he reached down a fat briefcase from the luggage rack. "You look bushed. About the way I feel. Sit down, girl. Put your feet up. Bad journey?"

"Not really." Remembering the disaster of his, she felt a qualm of grateful sympathy as she obeyed him. Since only the top and bottom berths had been made up, it was possible to sit quite comfortably on the lower one, and she leaned back for a moment and closed her eyes, only to open them again at the unmistakable sound of a popping cork.

"Not champagne," he said. "Second-class, that's me. Inferior substitutes only. Not a big rape scene either, in case you were wondering. Fact is"—he took a hard breath—"I'm mopy as a wet hen myself. My Sheila scrubbed me, back at Victoria. She was coming to Dubrovnik, for the ride. We had a bit of barney and she slung off. So—my tough." Holding the bottle in his left hand, he produced two surprising silver mugs from the briefcase and handed them to Julia.

"Lucky for me." She handed one back to him, so that he could pour steadily against the swinging of the train.

"Proper fool I feel." He filled his own mug and propped the bottle in the corner of the briefcase. "I was doing my nut till you came along. Now, my oath, I'm famished. How about you?"

"Ravenous." She took a fortifying swig of dry fizz. "I'm a fool. I thought there'd be a restaurant car."

"Always read the small print." Sitting on the far end of the berth, he delved in the briefcase and produced the most heart-rending picnic Julia had ever seen. The girl in the fur cape had had expensive tastes and Tarn Menzies had done his best to cater to them. There was a plastic container of smoked salmon, and another of olives: mixed black and green. There were joints of cold chicken with a faint tang of lemon about them; firm tomatoes and slices of Cheddar cheese flavoured with port. Handing her a pear, "No dessert," he said. "Pam won't touch it. Weight problems."

"I couldn't eat another thing." And then. "I am so sorry."

He shrugged. "No use whipping the cat. More wine? We can't recork it, and it should give us a good night." His laugh was harsh. It could hardly, she thought, have been the wine's original purpose. But she was glad of it. Combined with the good food, it was easing the day's tensions out of her. Only—a tiny alarm rang somewhere at the back of her mind—was it, just possibly, doing the same thing, rather too effectively, for him? Was there not something faintly predatory in the way those dark, heavy-lidded eyes were considering her? And if there was one thing she could do without, it was finding herself stand-in in a seduction scene. She must fend him off, tactfully, now, before things went any further. But how? Well: the wine glowed in her; there was an easy way. Nothing so convincing as the truth. "I'm sorry if I'm not very good company," she said. "I've got a lot on my mind."

"Tough."

The lazy unconcern of his tone goaded her into speech. "I'm looking for my son." After all, a son, usually predicates a father.

"Mislaid him, have you?" The dark eyes, wide open now, considered her quizzically.

"You could call it that. Precisely." Her own voice

was bitter in her ears. "I had him adopted. At five days old. It took me five years to realise what I'd done."

"My oath!" She had his full attention now. "Why? You did say—Mrs. Rivers?"

She had forgotten how it felt to blush. "Yes. But, you see, it was no good." The train hummed and muttered. The wine was strong in her. Did it feel like this to enter a confessional, tell all, and be absolved? "It was his family," she found herself explaining. "Breckon's. My husband's. Ex-husband's," she amended bitterly. "We had to live with them. He'd inherited the lot, you see. He felt responsible for the others. He said I didn't understand. But I did!" How often she had argued it with herself. "They hated me. All of them. Right from the first. Then, they started trying to kill me. He wouldn't believe it. Said I was crazy, like the rest of them. Well, I suppose it did *sound* crazy."

"Still does. Crazy as Christmas." But he was listening. "Where did this all whirl up?"

"In America. That's just it. You see, we met in Paris. I was there on a job. It was 'love at first sight.' " Bitterness put quotes round the words, and, as she spoke, she remembered how furious Sir Charles had been. "Breckon was American. French-American, from way back. They were Rivière, really, not Rivers. From Charleston, South Carolina. Soon after we were married he inherited the estate and we went back there. A great, big rambling house in the middle of a swamp. All the family living there. A very strange lot. Furniture from before the Civil War. Only they called it the War of the Northern Aggression. And someone tried to kill me. I fell in the river. Have you ever seen cedar knees?"

"Cedar whats?"

"Knees. Great big roots that stick out of the water, and saved my life. I hid among them, and held on, and prayed to God he wouldn't find me."

"He?"

"Or she. No way I could tell. They all hated me. It could have been any of them. Except it couldn't. They were all together, Breckon said. *They* said. And that was funny, too. His being there. Back from Charleston so early. He found me. Saved me, you could say." The half-voiced suspicion was one she never admitted even to Sir Charles.

"Tough." She thought he believed her. "So what did you do?"

"Nothing, that time. Except try and persuade Breckon to move into town. No use. He thought I was hysterical. I'd been dreaming again, you see. Nightmares. I used to have them when I was young. They stopped, when we married; then, at La Rivière, they started again. Worse . . . I used to wake up screaming. . . . I suppose it was no wonder he thought the whole thing was my imagination."

"But it wasn't?"

"No. It wasn't. Though, do you know, for a while, I actually tried to make myself believe that—believe he was right, that I'd imagined it all. But I couldn't. And then, of course, the fire settled it."

"Fire? Stone the crows, but you had yourself a ball, girl! Don't tell me that husband of yours said that was just another accident."

"Oh, yes. The wiring was a million years old. Everyone knew that. But what I wanted to know was, who drugged the nurse?"

"Sounds like a good question."

"It *was* a good question. Only no one answered it. So then I moved out. To a hotel. I thought Breckon would follow me. He didn't." Memory of those days of waiting, of the letters, the telephone calls all unanswered was bile in her mouth. "Sir Charles came instead. My boss. I'd written to him. He said the whole thing stank. In the end I went back to England with him. Well—it was a job. A good one. And, he said— Sir Charles—more chance for Breckon and me in London away from his family. If he came."

"Did he?"

"In the end. Too late. I'd started the divorce proceedings. In fact, I got my final decree the day after—" She felt herself blush again, remembering that one night of pure happiness; the morning's bleak aftermath. After the long silence, Breckon had arrived, unannounced, at the office, and swept her out to dinner and so back to her flat for that one night of the old ecstasy. Only, in the morning, as once before, had come the bombshell. He was, simply, taking it for granted that she would come back to La Rivière with him. And, trying to explain her refusal, she had heard herself, with a kind of instant horror, blurting out the admission that she had even found herself suspecting *him* when she was attacked there before: "We can't go back to that."

The words had died at sight of his face. "You thought I—" He had put down his coffee cup, reached for his jacket, and left her. For good. It should at least have cured her of loving him, but, unbearably, it did not even do that. When she discovered, too late, that she was going to bear his child, she had tried to hate him, failed, and, for a while, horribly, found herself almost hating the unborn child instead. Poor little creature. She would never forget the late, difficult, lonely birth; the quick, as quickly stifled gasp from doctor and midwife, and then their determined, intolerable cheerfulness. He was not only illegitimate, her little boy—he had a bad arm, too.

Tarn Menzies was quick. He seemed to get the bones of the wretched story from her incoherent phrases. "If it had been a girl," she said. "I'd have kept her. I think. Boys need a father. Sir—my boss said that. And then"—she drank the last of her wine—"it was a boy, and—like that. The doctors said I would never manage. It was going to take money, lots of money, for treatment. And—I'd refused alimony. I had to work. They all said it would be better for me, for both of us." She still remembered her shock of surprise when Sir Charles said that. "I gave in," she said. "Signed the papers. I'll never forgive myself."

"Tough. But when you changed your mind, surely you could trace him?"

"That's what I thought. At first. It was a blank wall. Oh, he'd been lucky, they told me, my nameless baby. A marvellous adoption. And one stipulation. Absolute secrecy. Well: fair enough. What right had I to know? I suppose that's what they thought. The adopters. In a way, when I found that out, I felt a little better. At least he must be in good hands. But now. . . ."

"Now?" he prompted, as she paused.

"God knows." She poured out the story of the

anonymous letters, the photograph, and now the train and hotel bookings.

"Queer thing about the sleeper," he said at last. "Did you confirm the hotel?"

"No." Doubt about this had been nagging at her. "But I've plenty of money. And it's early in the season. If they don't recognise my voucher, I ought to be able to book in there just the same."

"And then?"

"Wait," she said. "What else can I do? Until they choose to get in touch. If they do." She was dangerously near to tears again.

"You're tuckered out," he said. "And no wonder. Fill in those forms of yours and I'll take them down to the man while you put yourself to bed. Fifteen minutes?"

"Ten," she said. "And thanks for everything."

"My pleasure. I was pretty damned low myself when you turned up. You've done me good." He laughed his rather grating laugh. "I've not thought of Pam since you started your story, Scheherazade. And now, sweet dreams. Things will look better in the morning."

"They could hardly look worse."

He paused, with his hand on the half-open door. "No silly sleeping in your clothes, mind. Tonight, I'm a sheep in wolf's clothing."

"You're an angel."

"Thanks!" He quirked a black brow and left her.

Relaxed with wine and food, and the telling of her story, she was actually half asleep when he came back, and it was easy enough to pretend to be entirely so, listening to him make his quiet preparations and then climb into the upper berth. How lucky, after all, she had been. Thinking this, she slept, rousing occasionally when the train stopped, with the inevitable bustle in the corridor, but going off again, deeply, each time. At last, light waked her. Tarn Menzies had pulled up a blind. She looked at her watch and was amazed to see it was eight o'clock. "Lord, I've slept."

"Good." She heard him moving about above her, then a pyjamaed leg appeared, and he swung himself to the ground and reached for a silk dressing gown bought, she suspected, for this ill-started venture. Gathering up his clothes," "I'm off to the john," he said. "Ten minutes?"

"Make it fifteen."

Returning, he reported that they had acquired a breakfast bar in the course of the night, and they were soon lurching down the train to queue for croissants and passable, expensive coffee. They ate for a while in a curiously sociable silence, then he looked across at her. "I've been thinking."

"Yes?"

"I think you should go back home. I don't like the sound of it. Any of it. Can't think what that boss of yours meant by letting you come."

"I had to."

"But you said yourself you feel as if these people hate you. Enjoy torturing you. Have you ever been to Venice?"

"No."

"It's the kind of place anything could happen. Full of dark corners, and wet water. I don't want you to end up drowned, Scheherazade. Once is enough for that."

She laughed. "I wish you'd call me Julia."

"Thanks. But, seriously, why not pack it in and take the first train back from Milan?"

"And never know? You must see I can't. Not after the picture. He's real now. Dominic. . . ." Her voice lingered lovingly on the name.

"Hooked, aren't you? Just the way they meant you to be. Well, then—" He rose to lead the way back to their compartment. "Could you use a bodyguard? I reckon you could do with one."

"I beg your pardon?"

"I'd sure like a bash at it." He paused to let a fat woman hurry to her breakfast. "We were coming back to Venice after Dubrovnik, Pam and I. No reason I shouldn't switch plans and do Venice first. I'm an illustrator." He sounded as if she should have heard of him. "I'm doing a book on Venice and her trade in the Middle Ages. Dubrovnik's hardly changed at all. Can't say that for Venice, can you now? Might make sense to start there, get it over with."

"But your reservations?"

"No grief. I'll have to switch to a single anyway." His voice deepened with remembered anger. "My good luck it's early in the season. I won't get in your hair, word of a 'Strine, but I'd sure like to join your wild-goose chase."

"You think that's what it is?"

"Hope so. Safer that way." He pushed open the door of their carriage. "Goodoh, he's fixed it. Where did you say your hotel is?"

"The Da Rimini. Across the Grand Canal from St. Mark's. Do you know Venice?" At what point had it been settled between them that he would join her?

"Not well." He reached into his inside jacket pocket and produced a red travel-agency folder. "That's why it figures to start there." He selected a leaflet. "Mine's near the Rialto. Looks good and central. Far from yours?"

"Not as the boat steams. But are you sure?"

"As shooting. I'd be biting my nails for you. And besides"—his eyes glinted under the heavy brows—"what a gas—eh, Sheherazade? They won't be reckoning on me, see? They think they've got you there all on your little own. Lamb to the slaughter. And all the time, there I am with my sketchbook, watching."

It was undeniably a comforting thought, but reminded her at once of a conversation she had had with Sir Charles. He had wanted to hire an escort for her, but she had refused, convinced that if she did not go alone, as "they" had planned for her, they would never get in touch. She explained this, now, to Tarn Menzies, and he nodded quick agreement. "I should have thought of that. But no harm done so far. Just chance we shared the carriage. Right? Least I could do to buy you breakfast, and let you stay here till Milan. There we split. Should we quarrel?"

"I don't see why." She was remembering his scene with the girl—Pam—the day before. "We hardly know each other well enough."

"Too right. And too bad. Besides—no reason why I shouldn't go overboard for you. Every reason I should. So—at Milan, in case they're really watching, you ditch me, cool, quick and casual. Good-bye and thanks. Your reservations should be OK from there on, you think?"

"I hope so." It was curiously daunting to realise that she would not, after all, have his comforting presence at her side when she reached the unknown city.

It must have shown in her face. "Don't look so crook, girl." His smile was warming. "You ditch me, but there's no law says I stay ditched. I'm not a fool, see. And I'm over the moon for you. So—I've read your labels, haven't I? I'll phone you, every night, at the Da Rimini, and you go right on saying no, till you hear from them. Then you think again. No—" He paused, considering, "That won't wash. You don't want me cluttering on-stage just then. We'll have to think of a code. Let's see. Every night, I say, full of hope, 'Mrs. Rivers! How about lunch tomorrow?' If you've not heard from them, you say, sorry, you're booked." He stopped. "What the hell do you say if you have heard?"

She thought it over. "It's difficult. Because I suppose we have to assume that, if anything, it's my end that's going to be bugged."

He laughed. "No flies on you. Just that. I wonder where the telephone is at the Da Rimini. One thing: you'll know soon enough. So—more code. If it's in a very public place you'd better say you can't hear me, first time I call."

"Right. And when they do get in touch—if they do—I'll lose my temper and say I'm tired of being bothered."

"And I'll be round like a bat out of hell. Do you lose your temper loud or quiet?"

"Actually, I don't lose it much." Who was there to lose it with?

"Feel free to lose it with me." He was almost

uncomfortably quick, this young Australian, but she felt it made him a redoubtable ally. "When you do," he went on, "I'll be outside the Da Rimini pronto, ready to follow you wherever you go." He frowned. "I wish I could think of a better way to set it up."

But though they discussed it all the way to Milan, they only made a few minor improvements on this original plan, and she felt a curious sinking of the heart when she said her cool, public farewell there, and went off, by herself, to find the connecting train to Venice. Nothing wrong with her reservations this time, except that she was in a smoker already full of young Italian soldiers on their way home from training in the Alps. But their admiring glances, and comments meant to be unintelligible, were almost as good for her morale as Tarn Menzies had been. She caught the eye of the youngest of all, smiled at him, and found herself instantly embroiled in cheerful conversation. Extraordinary. And, thank God, there was nothing faceless about these friendly young men. They would never dart out at a girl from a dark street corner. Or would they? She thought of things Sir Charles had told her about Italy under Mussolini—about Mussolini's own death. The world's a jungle, Sir Charles had said.

Just the same, she was sorry when they got off, with many a backward glance, at Venice Mestre. For over three hours, she had almost forgotten her burden of guilt and anxiety, and now, curiously, whether because of Tarn Menzies, or of the friendly young Italians, she found that everything seemed different. Watching eagerly out of the window as the train moved out on to the long bridge across the lagoon, she felt, for the first time, that this was an adventure she was embarked on. She felt, amazingly, alive.

But in Venice, it was the rush hour. Emerging from the station onto a broad flight of steps, she was too busy pushing her way through the crowds to do more than half notice a bridge, a church, a great deal of sky, and, in front of her, the Grand Canal; and, immediately important, its *vaporetto* stops. Thanks to Sir Charles and his map, she knew that she needed Route Number One, bought herself a ticket, and sat down on a plastic green chair in a waiting room that rocked gently with the movement of the canal. Across from her, Tarn Menzies, on a similar seat, was leaning forward, eagerly trying to catch her eye. It was enormously tempting to smile back, but she would not let herself. She was here, now in Venice, as "they" had planned. How was she to know that they had not met her train? She made herself look cooly through Tarn Menzies.

He took the same boat, putting his case on the luggage rack beside hers and standing close to her in the crowd, but again she made herself ignore him. When he got off at the Rialto Bridge, she felt a queer little sinking of the heart, but ignored it and went on eagerly studying the buildings along the Grand Canal. Could the bars in the picture of Dominic belong to a second-floor balcony? No—stupid—there were trees in the picture. It was an outdoor scene. If "they" did not get in touch with her, she would spend tomorrow combing the canals in the hope of finding where it might have been taken. There could not, by the look of things, be many places where gardens ran down to the water. Just the same, it would be a long job, she realised, as the *vaporetto* went its slow and steady way from stop to stop, crisscrossing the wide canal. Because of the crowds on board, it was impossible to watch more than one side of the canal at a time. And the trip from the station to her stop at the Salute took almost an hour. If she heard nothing, tonight, she would decide tomorrow whether to hire herself an expensive motor gondola, or do her search the inconspicuous way, from the *vaporetti*. Probably best do that. How could she explain such a search to a hired gondolier?

The Hotel Da Rimini turned out to be more of a *pensione*, inconspicuously tucked away on a minor canal about five minutes' walk from the *vaporetto* stop. Entering by way of a trellised courtyard that would be vine-shaded in summer, Julia made a quick decision and spoke to the girl at the modest desk in English. No need to let "them" know she understood Italian. If they were really watching her. . . . She looked around. Several students, a family of Americans—it could be any of them.

Yes, the girl spoke English, and yes, again, indeed they were expecting the signora. She accepted the Acme voucher and Julia's passport but shook her head at her eager question. No, there was no letter or message. She summoned an elderly porter from his den to take Julia up to her room. It was in an annex, reached by a bridge that crossed both the courtyard and one of Venice's innumerable alleys. Temporarily disorientated, Julia thanked the man in English, gave him a handful of small change, and hurried to throw open the shutters and discover with delight, that the

window looked over the canal. There was no pathway
below. Remembering Sir Charles' advice, she considered
the chances of anyone's being able to climb in, and
decided, with amused relief, that it would be impossible.

By the time she had unpacked and changed, it was
after six. Almost time for Tarn Menzies' call. She had
noticed a tiny bar in a cubbyhole off the large entrance
hall that served as lobby, sitting room, and reception,
but when she got down there, it was empty and dark.
"A drink?" The same girl was on duty at the desk.
"Yes. Dry vermouth?" "Yes. If the signora would wait
a moment. . . ." Once again she summoned the elderly
gnome of a porter, who soon reappeared and shambled
over to Julia with her drink on a battered tin tray.
Sipping it, Julia looked around the deserted lobby for
a telephone booth, but saw no sign of one. Could the
one on the reception desk be all there was?

It rang and the girl answered it. "For you, signora."

"I take it here?"

"Si." The girl handed over the receiver.

"Hullo." Tarn Menzies' voice sounded deep and
reassuring. "Mrs. Rivers? It's that 'Strine again. How
about a drink and a bite of pasta?"

"I'm sorry," said Julia. "I can't hear you very well."

"Oh." She could feel him taking it in. "Telephone
in the lobby?" and then, again, carefully and loud,
"Menzies speaking. I was hoping you would dine with
me tonight."

"I'm so sorry," she said. "I'm afraid I'm busy."

"Too bad." He sounded as if he meant it. "Another
time, perhaps." He rang off, leaving her feeling
curiously forlorn. It would have been pleasant to have

dined and compared notes with him.

While they were talking, the lobby had filled up with a party of cheerful young English students, and Julia found her chair surrounded by them. Listening to their sociable plans for the evening, she wished again that she could have met Tarn Menzies, made herself finish her drink, and went out, firmly, for a brief exploration before dinner. It confirmed what she had already begun to suspect. Most of the minor canals were too narrow for the picture of Dominic to have been taken across one of them. It must have been taken either across the Grand Canal, or from the lagoon in one of the few places her map showed where there was no causeway. Unless, of course, it was on one of the other islands. The map showed her that Giudecca and Murano both had wide canals without paths along them. But, tomorrow, she would back her hunch and start to explore the Grand Canal.

At the Da Rimini, one was encouraged to dine early, and Julia, eating delicious pasta and looking round the crowded dining room, wondered if anyone was watching her. To her relief, she had a small table to herself, and propped her map of Venice against the salt cellar to study as she ate. It was logical, but depressing, that so much of the Grand Canal had no footpath. Naturally, the Venetian grandees who had built those magnificent, decrepit palaces had wanted immediate access to the water.

Two harassed waiters, one old, one young, were doing their slow best by the crowded room, and when Julia finished her apple it was quite dark. Once again, she remembered Sir Charles. "Think of them as your enemies," he had said, unnecessarily. "And take no chances." She went to bed, read Ruskin, and plunged deep into the old nightmare.

Two

SWAMP WATER was cold round her waist. The thought of snakes sent a slow, involuntary shudder through her. Hands that gripped the smooth, clammy cedar knees were turning blue. She dared not move. Huddled under the huge tree, she prayed the mist that had hidden her attacker would hide her too. But in the few weeks she had lived at La Rivière she had learned that mist low along the backwater might still leave its banks clear. To stand up would be to risk disaster. Her teeth were beginning to chatter, the noise seeming unnaturally loud in the dank silence of the swamp. She clamped them together, listening. Nothing. Not a sound since the first flurry of activity, when he had come at her out of the mist, and she had ducked the weapon, hearing him (or could it have been a woman?) almost instinctively, almost in time. Instead of her temple, the blow had caught the back of her head as she turned to run, slipped on a patch of mud, and plunged into the swirling water of the Cooper River.

It had caught her like a piece of driftwood, and she had let herself go with its current, wondering, in shock and terror, whether this was the end, whether she and the child she carried would be swept, helpless, down to Charleston, the sea, and certain death. But at least the river was carrying her away from her unknown attacker. She had let what seemed an endless space of time go by, before, feeling a slackening in the current, she dared, very quietly, to begin to swim, to try and edge her way through the mist to where, she hoped, the shore must lie. It was the river itself that saved her, tossing her up, like the flotsam she was, into the backwater, against the cedar knees, where she had grabbed, and held, and felt, miraculously, the suck of mud underfoot. How far had she come? She had no idea. Her attacker might have followed along the bank, be waiting up there, in case she appeared. And yet, how unlikely. If she had given herself up for lost, must not he (or she) have done so too?

She began, slowly and quietly, to pull herself up, clear at last of cold water and clutching mud. Lying under the huge cedar, she felt the blessing of sunshine striking warm on her back as she strained her ears, listening. A bird called. A fish jumped in the river. Crickets sang. Up here, as she had expected, the mist was thinner. At the moment, the huge trunk of the cedar must hide her from anyone above her on the bank. But if she moved?

And then, like a miracle, Breckon's voice, some way off, calling her. "Julia . . . Julia . . . Where are you?"

"Here!" Shakily, she climbed round the great tree, heard her cotton skirt rip on a projecting root, and stumbled up onto the dry mud of the bank. The river must have brought her far and fast. This was a part of the plantation she had never seen before. Once, she thought, it must have been drained and cultivated for rice or cotton, but now the jungle had crept back, green and lush and trackless.

"Julia!" Breckon's voice was nearer. How on earth had he got back from Charleston so soon?

"Here," she called again, and began to work her way down the backwater towards him. Its bank had once been a dike to protect the fields, and must, no doubt, have had a path or even a bridleway along it. Now, she must push her way through dense undergrowth, thinking with almost equal dread of snakes and of poison ivy. But at least she was alive.

He called again, impatiently, and all of a sudden, a new fear blacked out those minor terrors of snake and ivy. He was back so soon from Charleston. Perhaps he had never gone last night, but hidden somewhere in one of the derelict wings of the huge old house, waiting for the morning walk everyone knew she took. Absurd, shameful, inexcusable suspicion. Why should Breckon, who loved her, who had swept her into marriage—why should he try to kill her?

"Here," she called again, her voice shaking. It was true that the news of her pregnancy had horrified him. "We're tainted," he had said. "I thought I had made it clear." He had never used that tone to her before. "I don't know how I'll face the others. We agreed—I *told* you—we agreed when the last of the cousins was"—he had paused for a word—"hospitalised. No children. No more taint."

He had refused to tell the others—yet, and she had suspected him of actually hoping she would miscarry. But—it was impossible. He could not have attacked her. Not Breckon. It had to be one of the others. She had done her best to hide her bouts of morning sickness, but Breckon's sisters had sharp eyes. She had seen them, more than once, fixed on her speculatively, and had, indeed, invented the morning walk as a pretext for avoiding the all-too-sociable family breakfast.

And if Amanda or Fanny knew, then, no doubt about it, they all did. Since living at La Rivière, she had a whole new understanding of that apparently agreeable American word "close." The Rivers were a very close family. Amanda, the brightest, would tell Fanny, and Fan, inevitably, would tell Raoul and Uncle Paul. And then?

"Julia?" Breckon's voice was sharp with anxiety. "Where on earth are you?"

"Right here." Now another fear was uppermost. Suppose he still refused to believe her?

At last, sighing with exhausted relief, she emerged from the tangle of undergrowth onto a recognisable if disused path. And there, coming round the bend of the river to meet her, was Breckon, immaculate in the white suit he had put on for Charleston. It made her more aware than ever of her own damply filthy, clinging garments. Like all his family, Breckon cared enormously about appearances and had, indeed, confessed that it had been her own Dior image, so carefully constructed under Sir Charles' tuition, that had attracted him at first. But only at first. . . .

"Good God!" He saw her and hurried forward, arms outstretched. "Julia! What happened?"

"I was attacked. No! Don't touch me: I'm filthy. I fell in the river." She stood where she was, and became aware that she smelled. "It saved my life, I think. Breckon, take me home!" She had never called La Rivière home before. Would she ever again?

His answer made it doubtful. "Attacked?" No conviction in his voice.

"Yes. Attacked. I went for my walk as usual. Along the river. Under the live oaks. It was misty. You know how it lies along the Cooper. Someone was waiting at the corner of the avenue. I heard them just in time. They had a club—something—I don't know."

"They?"

"I didn't see. It could have been anyone."

"I suppose you mean Raoul, or Amanda, or Fan. Or Uncle Paul, maybe, from his wheelchair?"

"Breckon, I don't know *what* I mean. I only know what happened. They tried to kill me. I fell in the river and it carried me down to"—she looked back—"to here."

"I can see you fell in the river," he said. "As to the rest of it. . . . You need a hot bath and a strong drink. You'll see things more sensibly after that."

"Sensibly?" For a moment she was afraid she was going to lose control, to laugh, to scream, to sob. Then, almost mercifully, she felt consciousness going. The world darkened and spun around her. Shadows of trees and Spanish moss flickered across her erratic vision. Swaying, "Oh, poor Breckon," she thought, "how he will hate catching me," and fell.

Consciousness was a white bed, in a white room, in whitely air-conditioned air. A hospital. Solitude. Safety? Could she be sure of that? The door was ajar, held by a band round the knob. Suppose it were to swing open and reveal her enemy? She would not even know him—or her. And—she was incredibly weak. There must surely be a bell-push somewhere in this sterile room with which she could summon help. She moved her head feebly on the pillow, and saw it, hanging across the night table, which had been pushed aside from the bed. It looked as far away as the moon, but if it killed her, she was going to reach it. If she failed, that might kill her too.

What time of day was it? When were visiting hours? Or, granted that this must be a private room, might not any member of the family come at any time? As these thoughts scurried across the surface of her mind, she was fighting off the knowledge of what was the matter with her. She had lost her baby. Tears began to flow, silently, down her cheeks. After all the battle she had fought, to have it end like this. . . .

What a wretched business it had been. When Breckon had told her about the family "taint" and warned her that they must never have children, it had been, although she had not known it, already too late. Absurd, appalling misunderstanding. Oceans-deep in first love, she had totally failed to see that for Breckon, at the start, theirs had been merely a passing affair. What extraordinary gaps of meaning, she thought now, bitterly, lay between the American and English languages. If the two of them had spoken different ones, they might well have contrived to understand each other better. As it was, he had taken it for granted that she was modern, and on the pill, while she thought—in so far as she thought at all—that this rapturous exchange of selves was simply the prelude to marriage. As, indeed, it had proved. Breckon had asked her to marry him, sleepily, on their third morning together, and, sleepily, happily, she had said yes.

Over breakfast in Breckon's tiny, borrowed flat, the blow had fallen. Crumbling his croissant, he had looked up to meet her eyes, not happily, and she had been aware, for the very first time, of tension between them. "By the way," he had said. "I ought to tell you, at once, in case it makes a difference. No children."

"No—" She would not believe her ears.

"Children." He, too, must have been aware of the gulf that suddenly yawned between them, for his tone, as he explained about his family was more and more hesitant, apologetic, unlike him. The plantation was a lonely one, he had said, too far, in the old days, from Charleston for easy communication. All very well in the high days of Southern prosperity, before the Civil War, but afterwards, another story. The result had been generations of inbreeding.

"But that's ancient history," she had protested, still trying not to believe him serious.

"If only it were. Our grandfather and grandmother

were first cousins. Their children seemed right enough, but"—he took it in a rush—"all our cousins are in mental homes. Father and Uncle Paul were the youngest by a long way," he explained.

"Uncle Paul?"

"Father's twin. Younger than him. He's still alive— the only one of his generation, but crippled with arthritis, poor man. He never married. Wouldn't risk children. He lives at La Rivière, of course. It was he who put it to us, when Cousin Charles went off his head. About not having children. We agreed, then, the four of us, to be grateful for small mercies and let the Rivers line die out with us."

"But you're all normal?"

"Oh, God, what's normal?" It had not been an answer, and they had both known it.

The room door was being pushed quietly open. A hand came round to release the loop that held it in place. With a frantic effort, Julia turned in bed, reached out her own, shaking hand, caught the dangling bell, and pressed it for all she was worth.

"Dear, I am so sorry." Fan, carrying roses. Fan, carefully closing the white door behind her. Absurd to have panicked over gentle, delicate Fan, who was standing, now, roses forgotten, crying in silent sympathy with Julia's own tears. And yet—she remembered that cry of Breckon's: "What's normal?" Not Fan—not really. The youngest of the four, always an invalid, she lived in the shadow of her brothers and sisters, and most particularly in that of Raoul, a year older than herself. If Raoul were to tell her to come to the hospital, take a pillow, and. . . . Convulsively, Julia pressed the bell again, grateful that she had had the wits not to let it go.

"What's the matter?" Fan put the roses down on the bed and moved forward. "Something I can do?" Whatever had made Julia think of her as delicate? She looked huge—dark in her habitual black against the whiteness of the room. Threatening.

"I don't feel well." It was horribly true. Dizziness swept through her in waves, leading downwards toward unconsciousness. "If you could call a nurse?" she managed.

"I'll help you. Whatever it is." Another step forward. "I always nurse Raoul through his bouts. I'm good. He says so." She was very near now, reaching out to take the bell from Julia's limp hand. And at that moment, miraculously, a metallic voice sounded from a speaker beside the bed. "Yes, Mrs. Rivers," it said. "What can I do for you?"

"Nothing," said Fan, and, "Come," croaked Julia.

"Silly." Fan took the bell, oh, so gently, and hung it out of reach again at the far end of the nighttable. "I'm family. Anything they can do I can do better." But, surely, her eyes were on the door, speculative?

It swung open and a tiny red-haired nurse bounced into the room. "Well, Mrs. Rivers, am I ever glad to hear from you." And then, to Fan. "We said, 'No visitors.'"

"But I'm family."

"Never mind. Mrs. Rivers has had a bad time. Right now, 'no visitors' means 'no visitors.' Lovely roses." She picked them up, shepherded Fan gently but firmly from the room, and returned to stand by the bed, her eyes kind. "How do you feel, Mrs. Rivers?"

"Wretched," said Julia. "I've lost it, haven't I?"

Something clouded the clear blue eyes. Then, "Yes, I'm afraid so," said the nurse, whose lapel pin proclaimed that she was Miss James. "But no harm done. Better luck next time." Her voice somehow failed to carry conviction. How could it? Everyone in Charleston knew about the Rivers family. "Now try and get some sleep, Mrs. Rivers," she went on, "while I rustle you up something to eat. Your husband will be here this evening. You'll want to see him, won't you?" Once again there was something in her tone that Julia's tired mind could not quite analyse.

"Yes, of course." Supplying the expected response, she wondered if it were true. Might it not be wise to wait until she was stronger?

"Only if you feel up to it." Nurse James had read her thoughts. "We'll wait and see, shall we?"

"Let's," said Julia gratefully, and drifted off to sleep.

She woke in tears, her whole body aching with shock and disappointment. She felt void, useless. "Don't mind it." Nurse James was beside her, with a tray. "It's always like this. It passes. Now, eat your soup, honey. The doctor's coming around soon." She gave the room a quick, professional glance that passed it as fit for a doctor's inspection.

"Doctor?"

"McCartland. You must know him. He's been the Rivers' doctor for ever."

"Oh, yes." Once again, Julia's mind registered something a little strange about the nurse's tone, but this time her own quick sense of disappointment explained it. She did indeed know Dr. McCartland, who drove out across the new bridge to La Rivière regularly every Monday afternoon, to sit on the screened porch gossiping with Uncle Paul until the family assembled for evening drinks. Then he would stay, rather silent, over his one long scotch and water, small shrewd eyes moving from one member of the family to another, watching . . . waiting? If Fan was ailing, or Raoul had one of his unexplained "bouts," the visit with Uncle Paul was inevitably curtailed, but the drinks session was always the same, and Julia had hated it, particularly in the last few weeks, when she felt her secret must shout itself aloud to him.

And now, inevitably, he was to look after her in hospital. Helpless tears began to flow again, and she looked with distaste at the tray Nurse James had swung across the bed.

"Come on, honey. Try it while it's hot. I heated it myself, in the nurses' kitchen. If matron catches me, I'm a gone goose. So eat up, quick, before the doctor comes. It's the only way to get strong, and out of here."

"Thank you." Julia managed a watery smile, tasted the soup, and found it delicious. She was famished. When had she last eaten? "How long have I been here?"

It was the question Nurse James had been waiting for. "A day and a half. You came in yesterday morning, and, my, you were in a state. How come you fell in the river?"

Julia opened her mouth to say, "I was pushed," then thought again. "I don't remember," she said instead.

"Shock," said Nurse James. "Don't worry. I expect it will come back to you."

"And I've been unconscious all this time?"

"Yes." Nurse James spoke with her back half turned, moving towards the door to listen. "Eat up, honey. I can hear the doctor on his way, and I want that tray out of here."

Dutifully, Julia finished the soup and leaned back, exhausted again, her eyes closing as Nurse James picked up the tray. "I'll come by to see you before I go off duty," she promised. "Be good now."

Left alone, Julia lay between sleep and waking and listened to the slow progress of Dr. McCartland and his train down what must have been a long corridor. His voice, with its residual Scottish burr, was unmistakable, booming out from time to time, as, no doubt, he emerged into the corridor between rooms. Other male voices acted as respectful accompaniment and Julia thought, with a pang, that this must be a teaching hospital. There was pack of tissues by her bed. She reached for one, blew her nose, and resolved that she she would not let herself cry in front of the students.

But when the procession reached the door, she heard Dr. McCartland halt it. "I'll see this one alone today. Just you, Matron."

In her gratitude, Julia managed to greet him with a warmth she had never achieved before.

"That's better." He loomed over the bed, smiling down at her with that codfish smile of his. "That's very much better. That's what we wanted to see, isn't it, Matron?"

"Yes, indeed." Miss Andrews, the matron, was a tight-faced, gray-haired woman, and Julia, submitting to the inevitable examination, could understand Nurse James' dread of her.

When it was over, "Not too bad," Dr. McCartland

summed it up. "Not bad at all. We'll have you back on the old plantation in no time, Mrs. Rivers. Just what you need. Rest and quiet, good food, and no more walks by the river. You shook them up properly, young woman, I can tell you that. If young Breckon hadn't had the sense to bring you straight here, I don't know what it might not have done to them, the state you were in. It was sedatives all round last night, and I'm still not too happy about Fan."

"She came to see me." Irritation at his preoccupation with the family pulled her up among the pillows. "There didn't seem much wrong with her. I'd rather not have visitors anyway. Except Breckon."

"They'll mind," said Dr. McCartland. Then, at sight of something in her face: "Just as you say, of course." His tone was indulgent, as to a child. "For a day or so, till you're stronger."

"Until I say so." Julia surprised herself by saying this, and got an equally surprised glance from Miss Andrews. This was not, evidently, the way one spoke to Dr. McCartland. "Which hospital is this?" she asked now, amazed that she had not done so before.

"Not a hospital." Miss Andrews stiffened that ramrod back a little more. "St. Helen's Nursing Home. You're lucky to be here, Mrs. Rivers. If it had been anyone else. . . ."

"Oh, I see," said Julia weakly and watched them turn and leave the room. It made sense, of course. St. Helen's was Dr. McCartland's latest project, an enormously expensive nursing home for private patients just across the new bridge from La Rivière. The patients paid vast sums, and so did a handful of students. And now, too, she understood an odd phrase that the doctor had used. Breckon had brought her straight here. For her own sake, she found herself wondering grimly, or the family's? How horrible to think like this. And yet, how could she help it? And he must have loaded her, cold, soaked, and unconscious, into the back of his huge Cadillac for the half-hour drive. It hardly seemed the ideal treatment for someone in her condition.

In what *had* been her condition. At the thought, the tears began to flow again, and it was thus that Nurse James found her. "Oh, honey," she began reproach- fully, then stopped at Julia's question. "Yes, I was here when you came in," she confirmed. "You remember— I told you. I never saw anything like it."

"Was I wrapped in a blanket?"

"No." The girl's hand went to her mouth, and Julia realised for the first time how young she was. She made a quick recovery. "Poor Mr. Rivers was almost out of his mind with worry. He said he hadn't known what to do for the best."

"No," said Julia. "I imagine not." She pulled herself up a little further on the pillows. "Has anyone brought in my things? I'd like to comb my hair before he comes."

"Yes, indeed. Miss Amanda brought them just after you came up from the theatre last night. She wanted to come in—just for a tiny minute—and see you, but I didn't let her. She wasn't best pleased with me. Make my peace for me, honey, when she visits you? The Rivers are bad ones to cross." And then, colouring. "Sorry, I forgot you were one."

"That's all right." Something had upset Nurse James. . . . Something she herself had said? She was making rather a business of fetching Julia's alligator overnight case out of the closet and unpacking it for her.

"Beautiful." She paused to stroke the rich brown leather. "A present from the family?"

"No, actually it was a wedding present from my boss."

"My goodness." Awestruck. "How he must have hated to lose you."

"He did." Memory of Sir Charles and his fury was curiously steadying. In all the years she had worked for him, he had never once failed to believe what she told him. If she had said she had been attacked, he would have accepted it without question. As, in the end, he had accepted her marriage. "It's your affair," he had said, giving her the extravagant present. "And I hope to God it works out better than I think it will. And, Julia, if you ever want to come back, there's a job here for you, and no 'I told you so.' Assistants like you don't grow on every tree. I just hope young Rivers knows how lucky he is."

Did he? Julia was glad to let Nurse James comb her hair, but jumped when she began on the back. "Ouch!"

"You've got quite a bump there." The girl's fingers were gentle. "You must have hit something, falling." And then, holding a pocket mirror for Julia, "A touch of colour, maybe?"

"No, thanks." Julia managed a laugh. "I never use it. Haven't got any." But, with a critical look at the haggard face in the glass. "I do see what you mean."

"I could borrow you some," said the girl eagerly. "Mrs. Frankson down the hall has a makeup case like the Ark. Two of everything. She'd be tickled to death. . . ."

"No thanks." Somehow, she felt that Breckon must see her as she was. But at least: "Somebody washed my hair," she said gratefully.

"Yes. Matron said to do it while you were under the anaesthetic. It stank. We gave you typhoid shots too. And anti-tetanus. I bet your arm's stiff."

The girl was babbling. Why? "Anaesthetic?" asked Julia, then turned as the door was pushed open to reveal Breckon, his arms full of white roses. "Thank goodness, darling, you're better." He handed the flowers to Nurse James and advanced to kiss her, lightly, on the cheek. "How do you feel?"

"Terrible," said Julia, as Nurse James muttered something about a vase and withdrew.

"My poor darling." Now his arm was round her, as he gave her a real kiss, warm and demanding. It should have been comforting, and was not.

"You brought me straight here," she said.

"I should think so! The most terrifying drive of my life. I did it in twenty minutes. It would have taken hours if I'd gone in and called an ambulance. I didn't even know whether I *had* minutes."

"Well, I survived," said Julia dryly. What was the use of discussing it? "But—"

"I know, darling. Terribly bad luck. I am so sorry." He turned, angrily, as Nurse James reappeared with the roses in a vase. "Put a 'Don't disturb' sign on the door, like a good girl."

"Certainly, Mr. Rivers." If Nurse James was annoyed, she concealed it admirably. "I just came to say goodnight to Mrs. Rivers. I'm off now," she spoke to Julia. "Be good, honey, and I'll see you in the morning."

"Thanks for everything," said Julia warmly. "I'll look forward to seeing you."

"Goodnight." Miss James beamed back. And then, more formally, "Goodnight, sir. I'll put up the notice."

The door closed behind her. "Very chummy with the help, aren't you?" said Breckon.

"She's a honey. Breckon, why did I have to have an anaesthetic?"

"I don't know." Impatiently. "Ask Dr. McCartland. He'll tell you, when he thinks you're strong enough."

"Oh." She thought it over. "There were—complications?"

"Let's not talk about it tonight, darling. Let's just be grateful that we have each other." He pulled up a chair, sat down as close as he could get to the bed, and took her hand in his cold one. "God, what a couple of days you've given us! You'd have been pleased, love, I think, if you'd seen how they all cared, back home. They all want to come and see you, just as soon as you're up to it."

"Fan came today."

"Yes. Stupid of her, poor love, but you know what she's like. Those her roses?"

"Yes." Privately, she thought the crimson ones Fan had brought more cheering in a sickroom than Breckon's funeral white. But then, it was a funeral. Poor child. Poor three months' child.

"Don't cry, darling. It's all over now. You'll be better in no time. Dr. McCartland says so. He thinks we can have you home in a few days for a good rest. Now, when did you last have that, I wonder?"

"God knows." The whole conversation had been leading up to this point. "And, Breckon, I'm not having it now. Not at La Rivière. I want to stay alive."

His long, fair, intelligent Rivers face flushed as if she had slapped it. "Julia, you're not still imagining things?"

"Imagining?"

"Well, darling, what else can we call it? I. . . ." He hesitated and the flush deepened along his cheekbones. "I hope you don't mind. I told Dr. McCartland about those nightmares of yours." And then quickly, seeing how much she did mind. "I had to, honey, after the way you treated poor Fan. Practically having her thrown out . . . She was in a real state about it, until Dr. McCartland explained . . ."

"That I was imagining things?"

"Well—yes. Dr. McCartland thinks it's the cumulative strain of that high pressure job of yours. Lots of rest, he says, and no more excitement."

"Like being pushed into the Cooper River? You aren't suggesting I imagined that too?"

"Of course not, love, but—you could have slipped. And I can tell you one thing. I checked on that, too. I'm not an undercover man like your Sir Charles, but when it's my wife, I do my best. They were all together, the family, at breakfast. When it happened. Every one of them."

"Even Uncle Paul?" She regretted the question the moment it was spoken.

"My poor darling." He took it beautifully, his hand kind on hers. "What horrors you have been giving yourself. No. Uncle Paul didn't follow you down to the Cooper in his wheelchair and contrive to push you in. Yesterday was his birthday—maybe you had forgotten?—and he celebrated it at breakfast with the family."

"Oh, my goodness." She had forgotten. "And your father's."

"Never mind, love. They won't hold it against you. Why should you remember?"

"But, Breckon—" Exhaustion was washing through her, its waves higher and higher. She must explain, beg, insist. . . .

"You're tired out, love." He reached across her and pressed the bell. "We'll talk about it tomorrow."

Three

AT THE Da Rimini, breakfast began at seven thirty. There was no note for Julia at the desk, no message. Idiotic that she and Tarn Menzies had made no arrangement for a morning summons. And nothing she could do about it now. She ate rolls, drank surprisingly good coffee, and was back in her room putting Sir Charles' map into her shoulder bag when the buzzer by her bed sounded. Lifting the house telephone, she hoped for a moment that it might be possible to take an outside call up here, but it was merely the girl at the desk summoning her to the telephone in the lobby. Her heart beat hard as she hurried across the bridge and downstairs. Would this be her summons? But it was Tarn Menzies' voice, asking eagerly if she felt like lunching. "No." It was difficult not to sound too regretful. "I'm busy today. Sorry."

"I'm sorry too." Once again she had the comfortable feeling that he meant it.

It gave her the courage to start the long day of apparently aimless sightseeing, and she needed it. She had decided, the night before, to do two stops at a time on the *vaporetto*, then go back and study the other side. However tempted, she would skip nothing. The map Sir Charles had given her was undoubtedly the best possible one, but still might not be entirely accurate. The only way to be sure of a clear view from the boat was to stand by the rail that slid aside to let people elbow their way on and off. Inevitably, when the stop was on her side, Julia found herself in the thick of a pushing, shoving, surprisingly tolerant crowd. But it was exhausting work. She began by going up to St. Mark's, because it was the obvious thing for a tourist to do, in case that mattered, and also because beyond St. Mark's the map showed a broad causeway all the way to the tip of the island. No chance, surely, of the picture's having been taken there.

The map showed a garden between the two stops on either side of St. Mark's itself, but one look told her this was not the one she wanted. It was public, set back behind a causeway thronged with souvenir sellers, newspaper kiosks, tourists, and fat, unpleasant pigeons. She went on to the second stop, Santa Zaccaria, sparing a wry glance for St. Mark's itself. "Like the Brighton

Pavilion," Sir Charles had said. "Only with less excuse."

Just to be doubly sure, she walked back along the front from Santa Zaccaria, pausing first to buy an *International Herald Tribune* and then, as everyone else did, on the humpbacked bridge with its view of the Bridge of Sighs. But the idea of the prison to which this led sent a shudder through her. She had almost convinced herself that the bars in Dominic's picture were nothing more sinister than a garden balustrade. But how could she be sure? Last night's horrible mixture of memory and nightmare had left her more than ever haunted by the fear that the letters about Dominic were somehow connected with that terrible time back at La Rivière. But why should they be? Nobody there so much as knew of Dominic's existence, and, even if they had by some strange chance found out, what was he to them, bastard child of a divorced wife? The young lawyer Sir Charles had sent to see her in hospital had been ruthlessly clear about this. It had been one of the accumulated blows that had finally pushed her over the edge of reason and made her let the child (her Dominic) go for adoption. So—no reason in the world to connect what was happening to her now with the Rivers, or with La Rivière. Only, illogically, the feeling of hatred that had come over so clearly in last night's dream memories would connect itself in her mind with the sadistic behaviour of her unknown tormentors now. All imagination, of course; that imagination about which Breckon had so often teased her.

Why had he never answered her letters? She would not let herself think about it. He was very likely right: a clean break was best. She tucked the *Herald Tribune* into her bag and joined the queue for the Linea Two boat going down the canal towards the station. This time her two stops took her to Santa Maria Zobenigo, which, she saw, was where one got off for the Fenice Theatre. Extraordinary to be here in Venice, guidebook and map in hand, and yet only casually aware of all the wealth of history and interest that surrounded her. Just the same, with warm sun shining down and tourist crowds around her, she did feel herself, from time to time, somehow cheered and fortified by a glimpse of pastel-coloured courtyard; heraldic poles outside a pink palazzo; a garden with benevolent lions on its pillars. . . . But the garden did not have the right kind of railings.

From Santa Maria she made herself go back to her own stop at the Salute, though she was almost certain she had missed nothing on the south side of the canal. She was right. Getting off at the Salute to buy her new ticket, she was thinking angrily about the wasted time, when she saw a familiar figure. Tarn Menzies was sitting comfortably on a bit of wall, sketchbook in hand, gazing up at the solid grey bulk of Santa Maria della Salute. Should she speak to him? The only other people who had got off her boat had already gone purposefully up the steps of the church. No one could be following her. And the boat she wanted was not yet in sight. Yielding to temptation, she strolled across the paved terrace so as to cross his line of vision.

"Hi, there!" He joined her at once, sketchbook in hand. "I've had a weather eye out for you. Obvious place to start. Right?" A quick glance had reassured him, as it had her, that they could not be overheard. "Any joy this morning?"

"Not so far. But I've only just started. It's going to take days." As she spoke, she glanced at his sketch and wished she knew more about modern art.

"For God's sake don't look! It's nothing but a dog's breakfast yet." He put a defensive hand across the paper. "My mind's not been on the job. Couldn't help thinking about you. What you say: that it will take too long. Mind you, it may all be right as rain. They may get in touch. But. . . ."

"They may not. They may just be torturing me. But why?"

"You really haven't a moral?"

"Idea? No. I've been thinking about it all morning. Funny: I dreamt about La Rivière last night. I haven't done that for ages. Someone there hated me all right. But what harm am I to them now?"

"I haven't a clue. Look! There's your boat. Tell you what. If nothing shows today, I'll come play too tomorrow. I'll take one bank, you take the other." He grinned at her. "Not sociable, but efficient. I'll give the art another whirl today; tomorrow I'm all yours. See you here? OK? And now you'd better make tracks."

She just got her ticket in time to push her way on board the boat that was headed towards the station. Back to Santa Maria Zobenigo, watching the north side this time, and admiring a handsome view of palazzos turned into luxury hotels. A terrace where, in the summer, one would sit out and eat. But no garden—no railings. This venture was doomed. Could someone really hate her enough to do this to her, simply for spite?

The boat was unusually empty as it pulled away

from Santa Maria Zobenigo and she glanced casually across to the Salute bank of the Grand Canal, thinking that she must be about level with the Da Rimini. Then she stiffened and began quickly pushing her way across to the other side. They were passing a garden with railings. Too late, by the time she had got across, to see more than that, but she would get out at the next stop just the same and go back.

The *vaporetto* hooted angrily at a wandering gondola, shot under the long bridge of the Academia, and drew in to land. As she got off, Julia was aware of a familiar face beside her in the pushing crowd. No, two faces, smiling at her uncertainly, the Miss Browns from the train. "Lovely morning," said one of them, recognition established.

"We saw you up at the Salute," chimed in the other. "Marvellous, isn't it? You should have gone in."

"Not on the first day," said Julia quickly. "The first day I just look."

"You're not going to the Academia?" This, Julia thought, was the elder of the two, sounding shocked.

"No, bother it. I've just realised I left my dark glasses behind. That's why I got off. I've got to go back to my hotel and get them, or I'll work up a hell of a headache in all this sun."

"Too bad," said the younger Miss Brown.

"We thrive on it." Her sister was patronising. "Oh, well, see you around." They turned, guidebooks at the ready, and plunged off, flat-footed, towards the Academia. Julia turned back to the landing stage. Disconcerting that the Miss Browns should have seen her at the Salute, without her being aware of them.

But, of course, they must have been already on the *vaporetto* she had caught. Ridiculous to let herself imagine that they were following her. And yet, she would keep an eye out for them just the same.

This time she got a firm hand on the rails at the right-hand side of the boat and stood there, watching eagerly for the garden. There it was, some distance away, since the canal was wide here and the boat was headed back across it to San Maria Zobenigo. Railings, evergreen trees, a hint of green that might be grass or some of the ground-covering plants she had noticed here and there in glimpses of courtyard gardens. Behind this garden, a surprisingly low, long building, which must be fairly modern. She had Dominic's picture tucked in her guidebook. Yes, it *could* be. . . . A drop of sweat fell onto the picture. Her hand was shaking. Could she really have found Dominic's home. . . . Prison? Had this been what they intended when they sent her to the Da Rimini?

The boat had stopped, but on the wrong side of the canal. She would go on to the Salute and then walk back as near the water as possible and see if she could identify the building from the rear. She looked back, as the boat pulled away again, to try and place it as nearly as possible. Two canals below the Salute? Yes, that was right, and then a little farther on, towards the Academia bridge. It should, surely, be possible to find, even among the confusing labyrinth of canal and alley.

Alighting at the Salute stop, she had a quick eager glance towards where Tarn Menzies had been sketching, but there was no sign of him, and her heart sank. It would have been good to have his company, just in

case she was really on to something. But he must have
finished his first sketch and gone on, doubtless to St.
Mark's. It was good of him, she thought, to have started
with the Salute for her sake. She could hardly expect
him to spend the whole day waiting around in case
she came back.

Anyway, even if she did decide that this was the
place where Dominic was being—well—kept, she meant
to do nothing at once. Sir Charles had urged her to
go about the actual confrontation with the greatest
care. After all, as he had kept reminding her, she had
absolutely no reason to suppose that Dominic was not
the adored child of admirable adoptive parents. And
yet, a creeping up her spine would keep suggesting
that not only she herself, but Dominic was in danger.
All imagination, no doubt. All parts of the horrible,
overwhelming guilt she felt about Dominic.

She found she was hurrying, sweating a little in mid-
morning sunshine. Making herself slow down to the
usual tourist amble, she noticed a couple she had seen
before, up near St. Mark's. They were unmistakable
enough, the young man immensely tall and thin, in
orange corduroys, the girl, a head shorter, in a huge
red hat and one of those long white nightdresses that
made the young all look like failed Ophelias. It seemed
a lifetime since she had worn clothes like that. Sir
Charles had taken one look at her scarlet shift that
first day at the office, and written a blank cheque. "Go
and disguise yourself," he had ordered. In a sense, she
had been in disguise ever since. Odd to think that in
her scarlet shift, or one of the long, flounced skirts
Sir Charles had also banned, she would never have

attracted Breckon's attention. She looked down at her impeccable dark madras skirt and shirt. Had she, somehow, missed being young?

Ahead of her, the couple had stopped to stand on a humpbacked bridge, arms linked, and gaze down a small canal towards the lagoon and the further island of Giudecca. Passing them, Julia heard the girl's voice, plaintive: "But, Peter, I don't *feel* like pictures. Can't we do something outdoors, while it's so fine? You know it won't last." A trace of something in her accent nagged at Julia.

"But it's the Academy I came to see." His voice was straight BBC, but low, so that Julia, down the steps from the bridge, could hear no more. Surely, she thought, plunging into a darkly shadowed alley, this was an odd route to take from St. Mark's to the Academy. But then, for a tourist, the whole point of Venice was that one could wander, freely, with time no object and traffic no threat.

She was hurrying again. Slow down. Relax. Keep a cool head. She would need it if this was the right house. Here was the second canal. She crossed it and stood for a moment at a choice of two paths, one straight ahead and one leading along beside the canal, towards the southern side of the island. Obviously, she must go straight ahead, thus keeping as close to the Grand Canal as possible. Behind her as she started forward again, she heard the young couple pause to debate the same point. They must walk quite fast between stops.

This, she thought, was rather an elegant alley. She had already noticed how hard it was to tell, from their walled outsides, what the houses were like, but here there were high, handsome gates, a dolphin knocker, an ornate light over a doorway, and, ahead, the sight of trees over a wall, where, apparently, the alley ended. Could this be her garden, running, perhaps, behind that long, low house, as well as on the canal side?

There was no one in sight. Behind her, she could hear the young couple's footsteps coming steadily along. He had metal studs in his shoes, she flip-flopped along in rubber sandals. The alley suddenly felt dark, cold and far too solitary. A cul-de-sac, and the enemy closing in behind? Absurd. But she was hurrying again as she reached the closed gate in the wall and saw that, in fact, the alley turned sharp left along it. And, on the gate, a notice. This, it appeared, was the Peggy Guggenheim Museum of Modern art. And it was closed for the winter.

"Damnation," said the young man's deep voice. They had caught up and were reading the notice over her shoulder.

"It opens this afternoon."

Julia had placed the girl's accent now. No wonder she had felt that moment of illogical fright. Overlaid by years of absence, there was still more than a hint of the deep, melodious drawl of the southern United States. It took her straight back to La Rivière and all that nightmare. On an impulse, she turned to look up at the tall young man. "Have you been here before?"

"To Venice?"

"No, to the Peggy Guggenheim."

"Yes, to both. I'm just setting about educating this barbarian here." His tone and casual arm round her shoulders made it friendly.

"Does it have a garden running down to the river?"

"Yes." If the question surprised him, he did not show it.

"Open to the public?"

"Of course. When the rest of it is. You'd better come back this afternoon. It's worth a visit."

"Thanks," she said. "I think I will." And now, back to the Academia stop. It was wildly improbable that Dominic was living in a public art gallery. She would certainly not stop searching because of an outside chance like this. She started along the fork of the alley and, inevitably, the young couple came too. It gave her a chance to probe a little further. Was there, after all, something a little too pat about this encounter? "You're from the States?" she asked the girl.

"Because I'm a barbarian?"

"Because of your accent, nut," said the young man.

"Sue," said the girl automatically, as if she had done so many times before. And then, with a sudden, composed politeness, to Julia. "Yes, I'm from Savannah, Georgia," she added helpfully. "Only I grew up in Scotland. This is my first time in Italy. It's—out of this world. And am I ever lucky to have found Pete here to show me round. What he doesn't know's not worth knowing."

"Even if I do drag you off to the Academy?" He was tired of the conversation now, and as they emerged into a small square he put a firm hand on the back of her brown neck. "Come on, honey chile, or they'll close that gallery. Be seeing you." He dismissed Julia with the casual courtesy of the young.

"Good-bye." She felt a thousand years old as she paused to look in a bakery window, savour the sweet smell of fresh bread, and laugh at herself for imagining them anything but a young couple immersed in Venice, and in each other. But she would come back to the Peggy Guggenheim in the afternoon. There might be a private bit of garden. . . . And, right now, she must find herself some lunch. The tensions of the morning had left her suddenly famished, and she was glad to remember an unpretentious café by the Academia Bridge. It was already quite full, but she found herself a small table by the window overlooking the canal, and ordered pizza and a glass of red wine. She was tired, too, realising, now she had sat down, that she had been on her feet all morning. Restful to have to walk no further than to the Peggy Guggenheim after lunch.

"Hullo!" She looked up to see the Miss Browns standing hopefully over her. "Do you mind if we join you?" The older of the two suited the action to the word. "This place is packed. *And* it's going to rain."

"Oh, no!" This had not occurred to Julia as a hazard.

"Oh, yes." The younger Miss Brown pulled off her tweed jacket and settled it on the back of her chair. "And in Venice, when it rains, indeed it raineth."

"In that case," Julia was on her feet, glad, somehow, of the excuse to get away. "I'd better hurry home and get my mac."

"And an umbrella, if I know Venice," said the elder Miss Brown.

Huge drops of rain were splashing down as Julia turned into the now familiar alley with Da Rimini's sign at the corner. In the lobby, afternoon silence reigned. There was nothing in her pigeonhole. The torture would go on for ever. She would never find

Dominic. He was probably not in Venice at all. Up in her room, she threw herself on her bed, cried helplessly, and slept.

Four

"KEEP AWAY from La Rivière." Dr. McCartland stood close to her high, hospital bed and spoke low and earnestly. "Get young Breckon away, too. They're not good for him. Or for each other. Inbreeding. . . . Years of it. But he should be clear enough. His mother was a Scot, like me. A great girl. She died when he was born."

"But—the others?"

"Ha. Thought no one had told you. Second wife. Local talent. Too local by a half, if you ask me. No wonder. And no reason why Breckon should take the whole load of them on his shoulders. Cousins, semi-cousins and all. Persuade him to put in a manager for the estate and go back to that job of his. Have a go, there's a good girl. It's the best way I can think of to stop those nightmares of yours."

"If only I can." Her heart sank. Did he, too, really think the whole thing her imagination?

"You'd better." He moved round to feel the back of her head, gently. "Hard as that on the temple, you'd be a goner. Clever girl, you dodged and fell in the Cooper instead, and here you are. Right?"

"Right." She felt incredibly better. He actually believed her. And, equally important, she believed in him. This, she was sure, was not her attacker.

"And Breckon brought you straight here. Not to frighten the family. . . . Or not to endanger you further. Ha!" He had seen her face change. "Hadn't thought of that, had you? Get him away from there, I tell you. Stop him talking about the Rivers' 'taint.' Stop him thinking about it. And have another try, and good luck to you. The world may be overpopulated, but we can do with people like you and Breckon."

"Dr. McCartland"—the question had been niggling away on the fringes of her consciousness—"why did I have to have an anaesthetic?"

"Oh, that. . . . Nothing to it." But he looked extraordinarily unhappy. "A panic down in Emergency. Well—a Rivers."

"Why particularly?"

"You mean you don't know! The family put up the money for this place, that's all. What d'you think happens if a Rockefeller breaks a leg at Radio City?

It was like that here, when Breckon brought you in. Panic stations. You couldn't have had better care if you'd been the President of the United States, or"— he laughed—"the Governor of South Carolina."

Was he trying to reassure himself, or her? "Dr. McCartland." She had to ask it. "I did— It *was* an accident, wasn't it?"

"That you fell? But I thought—" And then he understood her. "Oh, you mean. . . . Oh, yes, believe me, Mrs. Rivers—Julia—when I saw you there wasn't a hope—not a chance of saving the baby. But, cross my heart, there's nothing to worry about. Not a thing. You'll have another, a great big bouncing Rivers to prove there's nothing wrong anywhere." And then, turning as the door opened. "Good morning, Matron. I was just telling our prize patient here how pleased we are with her."

"Yes, indeed. Good morning, Mrs. Rivers." Was Miss Andrews' tone always so acid, or did she, perhaps disapprove of doctors who visited their patients alone?

"Good morning." In her relief, Julia even managed to smile at the matron's frozen face. "I feel so much better today. I do thank you for all you've done for me here."

"Our job."

"Yes, of course. But you've all been so kind. . . . Do you know, I'm ashamed of myself now. . . . My husband's always said I was apt to imagine things. Everyone has been so kind, so, well, gentle. . . . You'll think me a fool, Matron. I thought for some reason that there was more to it than just losing the baby. That something had gone wrong." She got it out at last. "That I wouldn't be able to have another."

She smiled up at Dr. McCartland. "The doctor's just set me right. I feel a different creature."

"That's good." A quick glance flashed between matron and doctor, and there was still no warmth in her tone. "And lucky, too, that you feel better. Doctor, there's been a bad accident on the freeway. A busload of tourists and an oil truck. About as bad as it could be. They'll start arriving in about twenty minutes. Mrs. Rivers—I'd wondered whether to ask it—but if you feel so much better, don't you think you'd be up to going home, if we sent you by ambulance?"

"Oh—" She looked to Dr. McCartland for help. After all, he had just urged her to keep away from La Rivière. "I don't know. . . ."

He was studying her chart. "Well. . . ." He handed it to Miss Andrews. "Ordinarily I'd have thought a couple more days, but if it's so bad. . . ."

"Terrible. We'll need every bed we've got." It was settled. "Will you ring them at La Rivière, Mrs. Rivers, or shall I?"

"Oh, I will." She would persuade Breckon to take her to the Fort Sumter Hotel.

By the time she finally got through to La Rivière, she almost wished she had let Miss Andrews do it. First of all her own line to the switchboard failed to answer and turned out to have been accidently unplugged, then the line to La Rivière was busy for almost an hour. And when she finally got through to Breckon, he sounded distracted with worry. Fanny was ill. Nobody knew what was the matter. A fall perhaps? She had been found on the terrace, unconscious.

"Perhaps she was hit on the head." Despite the lump on her own head, Julia had still not managed to convince Breckon that she had been attacked. Like Nurse James, he merely thought she had struck her head in falling.

"Do you know, we had thought of that," he said now. "I'm beginning to think I may owe you an apology, darling. Uncle Paul thinks we should send for the police, just to be on the safe side. And I've got a nurse coming out to look after poor Fan. So if they really want to discharge you today, and you feel up to it, we could fix up a sickroom in the guest wing for the two of you. You'd be company for each other."

Half an hour later, Julia was in her own ambulance, being driven out to La Rivière. Her one, small comfort was that, getting out of bed to walk to the ambulance, she had found herself much stronger than she had expected. Instinctively, she had concealed this, subsiding with a sigh of relief onto one of the ambulance's narrow cots, but she now knew herself fit for any action she might decide was necessary.

When the ambulance drove up to the long, rambling white house, she made a point of seeming exhausted, and let herself be carried in at the separate entrance to the guest wing. "You poor darling." Amanda came hurrying down the long, ground-floor corridor to greet her. "This way," she told the men, "and quietly. My sister is asleep."

No sign of Breckon. Julia looked around the big, ground-floor guest room with dismay. French windows opened on to the screened porch that ran all round the wing. Anyone could get in, at any time. And where was the nurse? In one of the twin beds Fanny lay, sleeping heavily, doubtless under sedation.

"Here you are." Amanda stood by as Julia let the

two men shift her onto the second bed. "Nurse has just gone to get a Coke. She'll be back to settle you in a moment. You don't look too bad."

"I feel terrible," said Julia, untruthfully. The fresh air, even so little of it, had done her good. "I think I'll get some sleep too." She murmured a vague "thank you" to the two men who were obviously impatient to get back to the scene of the highway crash, which she had heard them discussing in vivid detail on the ride out. At least this was not a figment of anyone's imagination. It sounded real and horrible enough.

She opened her eyes, drowsily, after the men had gone. "Amanda?"

"Yes, dear." Amanda was sitting by Fanny's bed, doing the fine embroidery she loved. She now crossed the bedroom to whisper, "What is it?"

"Is it safe here? For Fanny," she hastened to add. "This wing's so lonely." It ran out among the overgrown tangle of shrubbery that Uncle Paul had let go back almost to jungle.

"Safe? Oh—did no one tell you? How stupid. They caught the wretched creature before you got here. A tramp, of course. He's been squatting in a shack we'd all forgotten. Down near where the backwater joins the Cooper. You must have scared him silly, Raoul says. He'd been there forever, they think. And . . . drinking." Her drawling voice registered distaste. "Uncle Paul thinks the fright you gave him must have sent him clean out of his mind. He thought everyone was against him, and attacked poor Fan." The suggestion that it was somehow Julia's fault that Fanny had been attacked hung in the air between them. "Then he tried to kill himself," Amanda went on. "Pills, or drugs, or something. He was out cold when they found him."

"How did they?"

"What? Oh, Uncle Paul remembered the shack. The workmen used it when they built the new bridge. There's a shortcut to it across the swamp. He only thought of it in the night. Lucky for that miserable tramp that he did. They've got him in the hospital now. Breckon went in with him. That's why he wasn't here to meet you. He sent his love, of course."

"St. Helen's?"

"Gracious goodness, no. The General. That's the place for tramps."

That evening the tramp died in the General Hospital without recovering consciousness. Breckon brought the news out to La Rivière, arriving at the same time as the night nurse, a tall capable-looking black lady whom Julia liked at sight. It was Nurse Morris who gave her the news of the tramp's death, since Breckon had inevitably had to stop to tell the family. "Mr. Rivers said to tell you he'll be right here," she said. "But I reckon, by the sound of those others, we've got ten minutes to fix you up pretty for him. They sure are full of questions." And then. "Well, no wonder."

"No?"

"I work in the General," said Nurse Morris. "I've a friend in Emergency. He says if that was a tramp, he's the President of the U.S.A."

"Oh, why?"

"We're not fools," said Nurse Morris tolerantly, tidying Julia's bed with capable hands. "He was black, so he was a tramp. Right?"

"No."

"No. You're British, aren't you? You've got

problems. We know that. But not like ours. So—you tell me what a tramp's doing with clean feet and clean fingernails." She shook up Julia's pillows briskly. "And only one puncture."

"Puncture?"

"The drugs, Mrs. Rivers. The shot that killed him. The only one he'd ever had."

Five

SUNLIGHT waked her, angling across her face. As so often happens in Venice, the rain had stopped as suddenly as it had started. She put a sleepy hand to her head to push back nightmare memories, and saw her watch. Only four o'clock. Still time to get to the Peggy Guggenheim Museum. Her madras skirt was crumpled from being slept in. When had she last let herself fall asleep in her clothes? She found its alternative pleated black one in the closet and was quickly dressed and ready.

The air was fresh after the rain, and the soft Venetian light more Canaletto than she had yet seen it. The short walk to the museum cleared the last shadows of nightmare from her mind as the sun dried the puddles. Naturally enough, really, that the tension of this sinister search for Dominic should bring back the shadow of that other time. When she finally broke down, after letting Dominic go, she had told the psychiatrist about her nightmares and he had assured her they were a healthy sign. She was working through the experience and would then be free to forget it. He had urged her to forget it all. Dominic. And Breckon. Lunatic advice. Build a new life, he had told her. Go back to work. Marry again.

Marry again! At all those meetings she had attended with Sir Charles there had never been a man worth a second look. Not after Breckon. And yet, now, when she tried to remember that dearly loved face, it was the dark-browed visage of Tarn Menzies that presented itself to her mind's eye. Doubtless the psychiatrist would call that a good sign, too.

The big door to the museum was open now, revealing a paved garden full of greenery and strolling people. But it was no use to her, since it was behind the gallery itself, and had no view of water. Indoors, the rooms were as crowded as one might expect on the first day of the season, but Julia was not there to look at pictures. She made her way, gently but persistently, through the chattering crowds to where wide doors and a flight of steps gave on to the Grand Canal. And, of course, it was hopeless. Even if Dominic had been there in the winter, he could not possibly be now that the whole garden was full of people. Besides—she took out the

photograph from its compartment of her big bag—
now she could see from close to it was obvious that
the ornamental railings were not the ones in the picture.
She had wasted her trip.

"Hi, there!" It was the girl from Georgia. "What
d'you think of it? Me, I think it's lousy. Have you seen
the family stuff in the basement?"

"No," Julia confessed. "I came right out here."

"I wish we had. We've done every mortal picture and
my feet are killing me."

"Barbarian," said the tall young man, with affection.
"Some of them are very interesting."

"If you like that kind of thing. Oh, God, Pete, don't
look now, but there's that drip of a girl from the hotel.
Let's get out of here, if you've had enough of your
damned collages."

"OK, Sue." Amicably. "They close pretty soon anyway. See you around—" to Julia.

"I expect so." She subsided on a bench, incredibly
tired, partly from disappointment, partly from the
heavy, unwonted afternoon sleep. She had half thought
of doing two more stops on the *vaporetto* before dinner-
time, but now discouragement overwhelmed her. What
was the use? It was undoubtedly all some monstrous
joke at her expense. If Dominic had ever been in
Venice, and the picture had been taken here, he was
probably half across the world by now. Nor need the
picture even have been taken here. Plenty of cities
had canals.

Depression washed over her in waves. It had not
been as bad as this since she had left the hospital.
Perhaps what "they" wanted was simply to plunge her
into another breakdown, a final one this time. But why

should they? And why should she let them? She stood up, squared her shoulders, and saw Tarn Menzies coming out of the big doors of the gallery.

"Bingo," he said. "I bet myself I'd find you here. Saw the garden from the *vaporetto* on my way down to lunch. They told me about it at the hotel. The museum, I mean. Does it look right to you?"

"No." Regretfully. "The railings are wrong. Besides. . . ."

"I know. Crazy place for it. Though, mind you, the help has to live somewhere. But if the railings are wrong. . . ." He looked down at her. "You look like three penn'orth of God help us. Come and have a drink. Better still, dinner. Why not?"

Why not indeed? The lovely evening had loomed before her with a curious kind of menace. She was not going to let them break her, but she was going to need all the help she could get to resist. She looked up at Tarn gratefully. "I'd love to. Only first I must go back to the hotel and see if there's a message." And change, she thought, and pull herself out of this slough of despond, and prepare for a good evening.

"Goodoh. I'll walk you back."

"No, thanks." Instinctively, she wanted to keep her friendship with him as secret as possible. "Let me meet you."

"OK, if that's how you want it. Only—how well do you know this place?"

"Hardly at all," she had to admit. "I've spent all day on the boats."

"That's what I thought. So where shall we meet that's easy? Got it! The Campo Morosini. There are a couple of outdoor cafés there, and a restaurant that looked good for a whirl. Here." He spread his map on the bench. "Over the Academia Bridge and follow your pretty nose. I'll get there early and grab us a table in the sun. Don't forget to bring a bit of warmth. We'll probably have to eat in, but good to sit out while the sun lasts. Right?"

"Yes, indeed. Oh, hullo." She had suddenly become aware of the two Miss Browns, hovering uncertainly by the bench. "You got here too?"

"Yes," said Miss Brown senior. "We heard about it at the Academia. Marvellous, that. The Tintorettos are beyond anything. You must go, Miss Rivers." As she spoke, she looked at Tarn Menzies with such patent enquiry that Julia felt constrained to make the necessary introductions. And, doing so, tried in vain to remember when she had told the Miss Browns her name. Absurd. She was starting at shadows again. What could be more harmless than the Miss Browns? And yet—their reserve seats had been next to hers in the train. . . .

Tarn was quick. Responding politely, he turned back to Julia. "Well, be seeing you, *Mrs.* Rivers." No reference to their date, but a reassuring glance to confirm it.

"I expect so," she said vaguely. "Must get back. . . ." And left him still hopelessly involved with the Miss Browns, who wanted to know what he thought of Miss Guggenheim's collection of modern art.

No message at the Da Rimini. Had she really hoped for one? Smells of food from the dining room made her realise just how much she had been dreading the lonely meal. The Da Rimini seemed to cater particularly to large parties of the young. It was no place to be alone. Was that why "they" had booked her there? To make her feel what she was . . . wretched . . . lonely. Well, she pulled a dark, uncrushable silk dress and matching jacket from the closet, thanks to Tarn Menzies they were not going to succeed. On her way out, she stopped at the desk to ask, once more, unavailingly, for messages and mention in passing that she would be out to dinner. The enormously fat manager was on duty, and an admiring leer paid tribute to the trouble she had taken for Tarn's sake and sent her out to meet him unaccountably cheered.

It was pleasant, too, to be beginning to know her way around at least this small corner of Venice and to find herself pausing automatically on the canal bridges to enjoy changing evening light at the end of each vista and think, oddly, of the long, skyscraper canyons of New York. The Academia Bridge was crowded as she had always seen it, but here, too, she paused for the wide view of the Grand Canal, stopped for a moment regretfully by the palazzo with the garden that she had seen, and dismissed, from the *vaporetto* that morning, and then went on, following her nose, as Tarn had said, round a couple of corners to find herself in quite a large square, with awninged cafés on one side and a rather forbidding-looking church at the far end.

The centre of the square was alive with children and pigeons, and she wove her way past a group of small girls on roller skates, who stood in a circle, supporting each other precariously, and giggling over some shared secret. Now they started off in a game of follow-my-leader which took them swooping and gliding up to the other end of the square, where the boys were congregated. The boys . . . Dominic?

But she had seen Tarn Menzies, standing up at his

table in the sun to wave to her. He, too, had changed, and looked more darkly striking than ever in light jacket and black, flared jeans. Two girls at a nearby table had been eyeing him speculatively, now stood up and moved away as Julia approached. "Hi." He had two drinks in front of him. "I ordered for you. OK? They take forever here."

"What is it?" She look dubiously at the fizzy pink liquid.

"Campari soda. Good for the digestion. I'll drink it if you think it's crook."

"Crook?" She tasted the drink dubiously. Then. "Nice; thanks."

"Goodoh. You look better, Scheherazade. My oath, but you look a right treat."

"Thanks." Something was nagging at the fringes of her mind. "How long since you left Australia?" she asked.

"Spotted!" He leaned back in his chair and gave a great roar of laughter. "I might have known you would. Bright girl like you. It's part of the act, see. Australian illustrator makes good. Besides, it's kind of fun, right? English as she is spoke is about as dull as a dog's breakfast—" He winked at her solemnly. "Whatever that means. Mind you, I'm the genuine article all right and tight. Outback . . . Geelong . . . the lot. Only, I've been batting round Europe since I was old enough to know which from tother. First I tried like blazes to lose the 'Strine; then I found I missed it. Hell of a time getting it back. Sounds phoney to you, does it?"

"Sometimes." Had she been mad to trust him so easily?

"I must get me a new phrase book—word of a 'Strine

I must." He smiled his warm smile. "At least it's a change from four-letter words. And that reminds me: any message?"

"No." She was glad there was none. She must have time to think.

"Thank God for that." His answer surprised her. "Because I've had one; my oath I have." And then, laughing: "Sorry, can't help it anymore. You'll just have to bear with me. Anyway, my blasted author is coming over from Ravenna tomorrow. Wants me to meet him and chew the fat. I wish to God I hadn't let him know I was coming here first, but there it is. Can't very well dodge it now, but I'll feel a hell of a lot safer if I know you're taking care. I don't like the feel of these people."

"Nor do I. But you must see I can't stop. If I get a message, I'll have to go, and, if not, I thought I'd go on working my way down the Grand Canal. After all, I've only got six more days."

"No law says you can't stay on. Afterwards."

"No, I suppose not." Oddly, this had not occurred to her. "But I wonder if there would be any point. Either they'll have got in touch—or not. And I should think I could do all the possible bits of Venice in the time. If I keep at it."

"Well, keep at it carefully tomorrow, for God's sake. If anything shows, save it for me. And if there's a message, ring me at my hotel. No, better still, I'll ring you in the morning, my oath I will. And if you've heard anything, Mr. Author Heyward can go jump in the canal."

"Thanks." It was heart-warming. Absurd to have given way to that moment of mistrust. "But I'm beginning to think I shan't hear. Ever. I think they're just having fun with me. Cruel fun. If only I knew why. . . ."

"Have another drink." He fielded a passing waiter and ordered them. "Julia, have you ever thought it might be your husband doing this to you? Ex-husband, I mean."

"But, why? Why him, of all people?"

"Why not? Love and hate are two sides of a dollar. And this sure feels like hate to me."

"And to me." She shivered and reached for her jacket. Putting it on, "I just don't know." She thought about it. "It was all so . . . so sad at the end. He felt he had a duty to his family. . . . Sometimes, since Dominic was born—since I failed *him* so. . . . Didn't do my duty by him, if you like; I've wondered if Breckon wasn't right. If one doesn't have to do one's duty. Regardless. So. . . . Might he hate me for refusing to see it?"

"You've heard from him since?"

"Never." Oh God, how that had hurt. "Not a word. Not from Breckon or from any of the others. Well, of course, I wouldn't have expected to hear from them. And—they didn't know about Dominic. So—no reason for them to write. Better not, really. I don't know a single thing that's happened at La Rivière since I left. Except"—she had thought of this often—"it never made the newspapers. So nothing too dreadful can have happened."

"You thought it would?"

"I don't know. I mean . . . whether it was just me . . . or the whole setup there. The doctor—McCartland—told me to get Breckon away . . . but I don't know if it was because he thought him actually in danger or just because of the way they all kind of batted on him. The money was his, you know; all left to him when his Cousin John died, in a kind of trust to look after the family. That's why we had to go back there, soon after we were married. Things were in a mess, Breckon said. He had to sort them out. But I had no idea he meant to stay, till we arrived, and there they all were, taking it for granted. I still didn't believe it; not at first. It was all wrong for him. Oh, of course he had to clear things up, but he's a whiz at figures; he said himself it wouldn't take long. But such a waste. . . . He could have made a fortune, Sir Charles said. One of his own. . . ." Her eyes blurred with tears. Suddenly, Breckon's face was clear before them, the fine bones, the deep brown eyes under fair hair that never would lie flat. How she had hated the way Amanda and Fanny used to stroke it into place for him. . . .

"Time for food." Tarn stood up abruptly. Had he noticed her tears? He sounded, suddenly, almost angry as he paid the hovering waiter and took her arm to guide her across the square. "Much too cold to eat out." He turned her down a narrow alley. "There's a place I read about on the way to St. Mark's. Sounds a bit of all right."

It was a big ground-floor room with a roaring fire on an old-fashioned hearth, and Julia, glancing at the vast menu that suggested still vaster prices, found herself wondering how well Tarn did as an illustrator. But he made her order lavishly. "And champagne, don't you think, in honour of our first meeting?"

"Two days ago." It seemed incredibly longer. She

drank the aperitif Tarn had insisted on ordering and wondered what had happened to the gay, almost defiant mood in which she had come out to meet him. Something, somehow had gone wrong between them, and the evening dwindled into a laborious business of manufactured conversation. Answering a stilted question about her work with Sir Charles, she found herself wondering whether Tarn was not perhaps regretting his involvement with her. Had he invented tomorrow's appointment in order to disengage himself tactfully from her search? It was a daunting thought, and she found herself, and was ashamed of it, consciously trying to charm her now silent companion.

"Sorry, girl." He smiled at her with a sudden return of warmth. "To quote from the book, I'm low as a shag on a rock tonight. The job's bugging me. And I'm biting my nails about you. I don't one bit like the feel of all this." He jumped to his feet. "Hang on a moment. I think I'll phone old Heyward and put him off. Do him good. No reason I should let him foul us up."

"Oh, please—" But he was gone, with a quick word to the waiter on the way.

Coffee and two glasses of strega had appeared before he returned, shaking his head. "No joy. He must be out on the town. Sorry to let you down, Scheherazade, but maybe I'd best meet the old bore. I've the worst feeling he's going to make a dog's breakfast of that book if I don't watch it. All my work wasted."

"How frightful. Have you done much?"

"Background. Before I came over. Plenty and to spare."

"Of course. Stupid of me." Was she stupid, too, to be trusting him? His quick changes of front baffled and disconcerted her. She finished her strega. "Do you mind if we go along? I'm whacked."

"Long, hard day?" He turned to summon the waiter, who had vanished, as waiters will when wanted. "Sorry, girl." He made a quick, efficient Australian scene, got a bill from the headwaiter, left what Julie suspected of being an enormous tip, and shepherded her out into cool night air. "Sorry about all that." He took her arm. "This way. The *vaporetto* will be the quickest. The Fenice stop is somewhere round here. Which reminds me. I thought we might give the opera a whirl. I've never been. *Turandot*, it's called, if that's how you pronounce it. Day after tomorrow. How about it?"

"I'd love to." Would she? Tomorrow, she would telephone Sir Charles; ask to have Tarn Menzies investigated. Mad not to have thought of this in the first place. Crazy to have talked to him so freely. Or—crazy to suspect him? After all, that scene at Victoria had been genuine enough. There had been three lines about it in the morning's *Herald Tribune*. "Girl injured in station fall." Poor Pamela had ended up in hospital with multiple injuries. Nobody would stage a scene like that. So—Tarn had to be genuine. His arm was comforting under hers. "Goodness"—there was a hint of apology in her tone—"how well you've learned your way round." He was guiding her down a narrow alley, darkly overhung by high, secret buildings.

"Built-in bump of direction. We 'Strines need it, all alone in the outback, with nothing but 'roos and rabbits." He was teasing her and she liked it. "Here we are." The landing stage at Santa Maria Zobenigo was deserted. "Damn, we must have just missed a boat." The landing stage, small and dark, rocked gently under their feet. From behind, footsteps sounded in the alley, coming towards them, not fast, but steady. Two men? Three?

Listening, she could feel he was listening too. "Julia, I don't know that I like this. Stand back. Away from the water. It's probably nothing. Imagination. Nerves. . . ."

Three shadows emerged from the alley and moved forward, their feet silent now, on wood. Faceless figures. The creatures of her nightmare. Tarn was fighting them, savagely, quietly, cursing under his breath in those unknown four-letter Australian words he had abjured. "Julia! Shout for help!" He went down as he spoke, and one of the shadows detached itself to advance on her. And, then, a miracle. A blinding glare of light and a water taxi sliding to a stop by the wharf. "Taxi, signor?"

As swiftly as they had come, the shadows vanished. Tarn rose shakily to his feet. "Thank God for that." He helped Julia on board. "Did you see them?" he asked the boatman.

"Muggers." The man spat into the water and started his engine. "I never see them. Where to, signor?"

"The Salute." He had a handkerchief to his face, and she saw the dark stain grow. "Do you believe they were muggers?" he asked in English.

"I . . . don't . . . know." Slowly. "But why? Why attack me? If that's what it was."

"God knows. Maybe you're doing too well. Coming too close. Because we'd sure as hell have been two dead ducks in the canal if this Galahad hadn't shown up. And, glory be, here we are." The boat nosed into the Salute wharf and he paid the man and helped her ashore. "Dead lucky, that's us."

"I'll say." She looked anxiously at the spreading patch of dark blood on his handkerchief. "Oughtn't you to keep the boat and go home?"

"And let you go back through those lanes alone? Not on your sweet life. I'm OK, Julia, word of a 'Strine I am. It's just a nosebleed, not exactly elegant. But I'm sure glad that water taxi turned up. Our saviour." Something she had not heard before in his tone. Rage.

"Yes. We were lucky." More than ever, his warm arm was a comfort. The alleys, so picturesque and full of life in the daytime, were terrifying now, heavy with the echo of those remembered, advancing feet. And yet here and there a couple stood in a darker corner, close embraced, and Julia found herself wondering what it would be like to be kissed by Tarn Menzies.

She was not to find out tonight. More and more, his arm in hers, she was aware of the rage in him. "Thank God you were with me," she said. "I'm . . . grateful, Tarn."

"Think nothing of it." Again that note of savage irony in his voice. "I'm just sorry I didn't give a better account of myself. The buggers. . . . Sorry, girl!" They had reached the door of the Da Rimini. "For God's sake take care tomorrow. Though, mind you, the more I think. . . . I bet it was just a random thing. . . . Muggers on the lookout for rich opera buffs. . . . But just the same. . . ."

"I know. I can't help wondering. But why?"

"I can't think. So—probably just our bad luck. Only,

for my sake, and your own, Julia, stay in the open tomorrow? With the crowds?"

"Believe me, I will. And—thank you again, Tarn. You're sure you're all right?"

"For God's sake, yes! A bloody nosebleed." With an obvious effort, he managed a lighter note. "Fine hero I'd make. Night, girl. Pleasant dreams."

Pleasant dreams! Fear walked with her back into the Da Rimini. In the lobby, a lively group of young people were making plans for the next day. A tall young man was quietly strumming a guitar; at the desk, a girl in a long grey smock was carrying on an endless, cheerful telephone conversation with someone, by the sound of it, in England. In all the lonely years, Julia had never felt so completely isolated. If the telephone had been free, she thought she would have called Sir Charles. As it was, she picked up her key and went upstairs, fear beside her.

She crossed the outside bridge, put the key in her own lock, and felt the ghosts lying in wait for her in the darkened room. Fear and depression. The old enemies. At least, after all this time, she knew how to fight them. All the lights on. Then, meticulously, carefully, she undressed, hung away her clothes, brushed her teeth, and made ready for the night, each habitual gesture a conscious effort. At last, wondering if she dared turn off the light, she remembered that the one from the bridge shone in through inadequate curtains, and made herself do it. Then, lying very still, as the psychiatrist had taught her, she began to try and relax, was convinced it was impossible, then began to drift. . . . Surfacing for a moment, she had time for one thought. Surely, at least, after tonight, she knew she could trust Tarn. Comforted by this, at last, she slept.

Six

"CHRIST! That imagination of yours!" Breckon's eyes shone with anger; his fair hair was rumpled where he had run an angry hand through it; a little colour, pure rage, tinted his fine-drawn cheekbones. "So maybe it *wasn't* a tramp attacked you both." His voice rose for a moment, then sank again to the whisper that so exacerbated the argument. He looked quickly across to the other bed, where Fanny still slept. "What does it prove? God knows there are enough lunatic students running wild. A scared kid, I expect, who frightened himself as much as he did you."

"Did they find the hypodermic? The one that killed him?"

"I don't know." Impatiently. "That's the cops' affair. Julia, will you for God's sake stop making like Sir Charles' assistant and make some sense? Things are bad enough without you acting crazy. Amanda's not a bit well, and I think Raoul is in for one of his bouts. And poor Fanny. . . ." He moved over to look down at his half-sister.

"Nurse Morris doesn't think there's much wrong with her."

"Nurse Morris! Trouble-making bitch. I ought to fire her for upsetting you so."

"Breckon, she didn't upset me. She just told me what's going on. Which is more than anyone else has."

"I'm sorry, honey. I know it must seem I've neglected you since you got back, but you must see how busy I've been. The servants are in a panic, God knows why. I thought for a while they were going to quit in a body." He looked at his watch. "Time you were asleep. Where's that damned nurse?"

"Breckon, she's only been gone fifteen minutes. It's not long to get supper." Or long to talk to your wife, she thought, but did not say.

"I'm sorry, love." He could still read her mind. "I'm bushed, is the truth. No sleep last night, and not much the night before. And all this . . . I wish Cousin John hadn't died."

"My God, so do I. Breckon, please, let's get away from here. Just as soon as we can."

"We can't." Whispering, his voice cracked. "Don't you see, love, this is my job. I'm *responsible* for them all. I've got to stay here, and cope. If only you'd help me."

"Oh, God." Her head felt heavy as lead on the pillow. "Breckon, I'm too tired. . . ."

"Of course you are, love. Ah." With relief. "There you are, Nurse." He bent to kiss Julia. "Sleep well, darling. Better in the morning."

"Thanks." Would she be alive in the morning?

"Sorry I was so long." Nurse Morris moved briskly about the room, settling things for the night. "Chaos in the kitchen. What's with the staff?"

"I don't know. My husband said something."

"Scared silly. You'd think we were back in the Dark Ages: voodoo, mumbo-jumbo, the lot. Took me all this time to get some chicken creole soup. Strongest I ever tasted." She was looking down at Fanny. "She doesn't look dangerous to me."

"It's her they're afraid of?"

"And the other one. Miss Amanda. Nothing wrong with her that I can see but nerves. Odd family though?" It was a question.

"Yes." Disloyal to say so. "I only met them two months ago." It seemed two ages, and, looking back, seemed also incredible that a mere two months should have shown such a disastrous slump in her relations with Breckon.

"I see." She sounded as if she saw a great deal. "That brother-in-law of yours looks as if he was set to tie one on tonight."

"To—?"

"Sorry! Don't speak the language yet, do you? Well, no wonder. Mr. Raoul's been drinking solidly ever since

I got here. Straight bourbon—no ice, no soda, no nothing."

"Oh!" It all fell into place for Julia. "That's what his 'bouts' are?"

"Seems so. Here, you're not supposed to get out of bed!"

"Oh, yes, I am." Julia was on her feet. "I'm going to have a bath." She moved over to the half-open door of the private bathroom, then turned back. "Nurse—"

"Yes?"

"I'm not such a poor thing as I've been letting on. You've seen the family. Do you wonder I'm lying low? So, keep my secret?"

"Sure thing." She yawned and laughed all at once. "I thought it was funny, an upstanding girl like you acting half-dead just for a miscarriage. Well"—she had seen Julia's expression—"I know, dear, but it's not the end of the world, is it? So you go ahead and have your bath—only don't lock the door, just in case— and I'll fix up sleeping beauty here. She's not had her pills yet. And then, thank God for a good night's sleep. I'm bushed."

Lying in the blissful bath, Julia thought it an odd admission for a night nurse. But then, she remembered, Nurse Morris must have come straight from the General Hospital. When did the poor girl sleep?

Emerging at last, she found the answer all too obvious. Nurse Morris was sitting in the room's one easy chair legs up on a stool, breathing deep and heavily, fast asleep.

Too fast asleep? Julia felt as if Sir Charles was at her elbow, pointing out the classic symptoms he had described so often. "Strongest soup I ever tasted," the girl had said. Her highly seasoned chicken creole soup might have contained any drug, and she would not have noticed. Why should she have? Night nurses do not expect to be drugged before going on duty. Julia moved over to the door and found it had no lock. Why should it? She propped a chair under the knob and went back to Nurse Morris.

"Nurse!" She shook her, hard. "Nurse!" No response. She looked round the room. No telephone. The curtained window spoke of the dark evergreen shubbery outside. And, inevitably, it would be from outside that danger would come. It must not seem like anything to do with the family. She turned off the overhead light and went over to pull up a careful corner of curtain and look at the catch of the French windows. A nothing. A triviality. She herself could have opened the long windows with a toothpick. Well, no, with a nail file. Thinking like Sir Charles, she began to feel like him. Competent.

And about time too. She was alone, in this dangerous house, with two drugged women, and someone had plans for them all. She looked at her watch. Half past eleven. Surely nothing would happen for a while yet? The enemy would not know how long the drug would take to affect Nurse Morris, and would also, surely, be allowing for the sedatives she herself and Fanny were supposed to take. That reminded her of something. She crossed the room and saw the two torpedo-shaped pills still in the saucer on Fanny's bedside table. The nurse must have passed out cold the minute she was alone. An appallingly strong dose of whatever it was, and the sooner she had help the better. Julia thought of the long, dark corridor that linked this isolated wing with the rest of the house. She was almost convinced that danger, when it came, would come from outside, but could she be sure of it? Dared she risk leaving the two other women alone? Somehow, illogically, decisive was the fact that she had no clothes but her chiffon nightgown and negligée.

She began to shake Fanny. "Fan! Fan dear, wake up!" So far as she knew, Fanny had taken no medicine of any kind since she herself had got back, and certainly her sleep now seemed light and natural enough.

She turned over, grunted sleepily, then opened her eyes. "What's the matter?" Her voice was reassuringly as near normal as usual. She merely sounded, predictably, cross.

"Fan, dear, the nurse is sick. I can't get her to wake up. Can you give me a hand with her?"

"Who? Oh—" She looked across at the slumped figure in the chair. "Why bother? She'll sleep it off."

It was bafflingly logical. Time was seeping past. The others would be in bed by now. Yes. She moved across the room to peer out once more, cautiously, from behind the curtains. The lights in the main house were all out. Was someone, over there, watching from a darkened room to see when their light, too, went out? No, the enemy would not wait for that. They might well expect Nurse Morris to fall asleep as she had, leaving the light on.

"Come on, Fan." She picked up the dressing gown from the foot of Fanny's bed. "We really do have to wake her." And then, an inspiration. "Raoul told me to."

"Raoul? Why?" But she stretched out an obedient arm and took the dressing gown.

"I don't know." Which, God knew, was true enough. "He just said so. She's on duty. She oughtn't to be asleep."

"Of course not." Fanny got quite briskly out of bed, swayed for a minute, then finished putting on her dressing gown. "Naughty." She looked at Nurse Morris, then surprised Julia by slapping her quite hard on one cheek. The nurse stirred a little, and Fanny slapped her on the other cheek. "Very naughty." The girl stirred again and muttered something.

"Aren't you clever?" said Julia. "Let's see if we can get her on to her feet, shall we, and make her walk? That ought to wake her."

"Yes. Must wake her." Fanny slapped the nurse a little harder and Julia realised with a qualm that she was enjoying herself.

"Come on, then." She took the chair away from under the doorknob, opened the door, and looked cautiously down the corridor. There should have been a light burning. Instead, there was blackness, and a smell of smoke. Fire. Why had she not thought of that? The ideal "accident." Three drugged women incapable of saving themselves, and, probably, no evidence by morning. She had often heard the family discussing the need for rewiring the whole place, and the prohibitive expense of it. This old wing was built entirely of wood, and there had been no rain for weeks. Impossible to tell from which of the rooms that lay between them and the main building the smoke was coming, but its increasing volume warned her that there was no time to be lost. Not a hope of getting Nurse Morris down that long corridor, which might at any moment become a hall of fire. She must get them out on the porch and pray that whoever had set the fire had not stayed to watch it. Surely they would be elsewhere, establishing an alibi, just in case?

She shut the door behind her and saw with relief that the nurse had responded a little more to Fanny's continued rhythmic, ruthless slapping. "We've got to get out of here," she said. "The wing is on fire. The wiring must have gone at last." She paused. If she drew the curtains and opened the French windows, it would be to announce to anyone watching that someone was awake in here. She dared not risk it. On the other hand if she turned out the light it would also tell a possible watcher that someone was awake. It was the lesser risk. If she could get them out in the dark.

She remembered something. "Fan, have you got your flashlight?"

"Of course." Fanny was terrified of the dark and always had one by her bed. She stopped slapping the nurse and went to fetch it from the drawer of her bedside table, and as she picked it up the light went out. She screamed, but to Julia's passionate relief, a small circle of light, flickering wildly, showed that she had not dropped the flashlight.

"The power must have gone." It was the one thing she had not thought of, but the enemy would have. "We must hurry. Turn the beam on the window, Fanny, and I'll get it open." She kept her voice calm, and the wavering beam of the flashlight steadied on the windows. When she opened them, she heard the fire, crackling merrily, a few windows down. "No!" She had turned to see Fanny coming towards her, flashlight in hand, bent on escape. "We've got to save Nurse Morris, Raoul said so; don't you remember?" She snatched the flashlight from Fanny's hand and pulled her back to the chair where the nurse had slumped down again, breathing stertorously. "Fire!" she shouted. "Fire, Nurse Morris! We've got to wake the patients." And then, to Fanny, "Come on, Fan, get your arm under hers. Now: one, two, three—up!" They pulled together and as the girl came out of the chair, Julia felt her make a feeble effort to help. "That's it." The flashlight in her left hand lighted their staggering ways toward the open windows. The sound of the fire, loud and close now, told her that she had no choice of direction on the screened porch. They must go away from the house, to the door at the end, and chance what might be waiting for them in the tangle of shrubbery below.

The French windows were too narrow for three, and leading the way, Julia thought for a moment that they would never get Nurse Morris through them. But Fanny had seen the glow of the fire now. Fanny was terrified and pushed the nurse over the threshold into Julia's arms. Then, emerging herself, she ran, screaming along the porch into the darkness.

"Hold up, Nurse," said Julia desperately as the girl slumped against her. "We've got to get the patients out," she said again.

It was the call of duty, and, as she had hoped, the nurse responded by stiffening a little. "Which way?" The words came out blurred.

"Come!" Now Nurse Morris was taking her own staggering steps along the verandah. If anyone was waiting at the far end, the two of them must be clearly silhouetted against the fire. Fanny had stopped screaming. What did that mean?

Behind them, the fire was roaring now. Julia raised her voice to shout above it. "Fanny, where are you? Breckon, hurry! This way, Nurse!" If there was someone waiting, they must think they had three conscious women to deal with. Unless, as she horribly feared, they had already dealt with Fanny? But, no, there at the corner of the porch where the stairs went down was Fanny, clinging to the newel post, gazing down at the black mass of the shrubbery below. There had once been a path winding through it, Julia knew, taking an ornamental route among azalea bushes back to the main carriage sweep, but tangling wisteria and wild grapevines had gone far to close it. Not much chance of getting Nurse Morris along it, even if Fanny *was* prepared to help. And she dared not try and skirt the edge of the verandah for fear of the fire.

Fanny was pulling her hand. "The back way."

"Back way?"

"Servants' path. Shortcut to their quarters. Come on!" Firelight, much nearer now, showed her face shiny with terror.

"Which way?" Between them, they were getting the nurse awkwardly down the steps, and Julia realised with a sigh of relief that Fanny's fear of that dark shrubbery would keep her with them. She was afraid, too; horribly afraid of what might be waiting for them there in the darkness, but just the same, they must lose no time. Far too dangerous to stay where they were.

The back path circled the end of the verandah, and they rounded it just in time. Flames were pouring up out of the end windows now, and a series of crashes told that the middle of the building was falling in. But luckily the path left the building at once, cutting a fairly well-trodden swathe through the bushes towards the black loom of the servants' wing at the back of the house. No lights there. But surely, Julia thought, someone, soon, must be wakened by the noise of the fire. "Hurry!" she urged Fanny. In her own desperation, she had so far not thought of the threat the fire presented to the rest of the house. Now, anxiously looking back as they turned away from the guest wing, she saw that the wind was fanning the flames away from the main building. It gave them a breathing space, but that was all.

It was dark in the bushes, despite the glow of the fire, and the path only just held the three of them, staggering along, awkwardly linked, their faces slashed by trailing creepers in the darkness. One of them lashed across both Julia's face and the nurse's. "What's the matter?" The girl's voice was almost normal, and Julia felt her pull herself together.

"The house is on fire," said Julia. "Hurry!" And, as she said it, heard movement in the bushes behind them. Someone had been waiting on the narrow path that led to the front of the house. Someone who had thought, quite rightly, that she would not know of this path. And, now, was trying to catch them with more speed than secrecy. "Hurry!" she said again. And then, "Fanny! I can manage now. You run ahead and give the alarm. Quick! Think of Raoul. He might be burned in his bed. And, look, it's lighter now."

It was indeed. The whole centre of the guest wing had fallen in with a roar and the windowless back wall that had once given on to the slaves' quarters no longer sheltered them from the light and heat of the fire. Incredible that the servants who slept nearest the guest wing had not wakened. Then, horribly, Julia thought she understood. They must have had that strong creole soup, too. "Run, Fanny!" she cried. "Wake them. Wake everyone. Quick!"

Nurse Morris had caught the infection and was trying to hurry on feet that still did not quite obey her. She tripped and almost fell, supported by Julia's firm arm. Behind them, the noise of pursuit was much nearer. The unknown enemy must almost have reached their path. When he did, he would be upon them.

Fanny was clear away. But who would believe Fanny? "Hurry!" Julia said again, and then almost stopped in her tracks at the wail of a siren. Thank God. Someone must have waked and reported the fire. And, miraculously, the siren was sounding from the service road that led to the back entrance, which was, come to think of it, the quickest way from the new bridge. "Help!" she shouted, knowing it useless, but hoping the pursuer might not. "This way!" And then, "Come on, Nurse we're almost there."

Behind them, the sounds of pursuit ceased suddenly. To the right, and ahead, the siren rose to its highest note, then cut off with a scream of brakes. The fire engine had arrived. She could hear the shouts of firemen as they leapt down and got to work, and now, at last, saw lights begin to show on the dark bulk of the servants' wing. Whoever had summoned the firemen must be waking the servants, or trying to.

Another siren sounded from somewhere down near the bridge as Julia and the nurse emerged at last on to the drive behind the servants' quarters. Feeling its shells crunch beneath her feet, Julia felt safe at last. But for how long? The firemen were desperately busy running out their hoses. Fanny had disappeared. And, worst of all, Nurse Morris was beginning to give way, her temporary flicker of consciousness exhausted. Julia, too, was feeling the inevitable reaction from the long, desperate day. Incredible that this morning she had been in St. Helen's, mourning her miscarriage. The nurse slumped to the ground. They were still in the shadow of the bushes. And, somewhere behind her on the path, she heard stealthy movement, very quiet now, very careful, coming their way.

The second siren blasted towards them and an ambulance surged out of the darkness, its lights picking up the nurse's inert figure. It stopped beside them, and the world swung giddily around Julia. Absurd to faint, now, from sheer relief.

"What gives?" Two men had jumped out, and one had her by the arm while the other bent over the nurse. Behind her, the silence in the shrubbery was absolute. And here was escape. Instant, certain escape. "The fumes. . . ." She let herself sway to that dizzy movement of everything. "We were in there." No need even to point to the blazing wing, where the firemen were now so busy. "I'm worried about her. Terrible time getting her out."

"I should think so," said the man who was bending over the nurse. "She's in a bad way. Nurse Morris." Of course. He would know her. "No time to lose. You coming?" And then, almost as an afterthought. "Anyone else hurt?"

"No." Fanny was safe enough. "Yes, I'm coming." Her teeth were chattering. With cold? With fright? With exhaustion?

"Here!" The second man had fetched a blanket from

the ambulance and wrapped it round her shoulders.
"In you get."

"I think I'm going to faint." She let him help her
up. "I'm all right—really. But she needs help. Quick.
I think she's been drugged."

"Drugged?" said one, and, "That figures," said the
other. They were the last words Julia remembered.

Seven

BRUSHING HER hair, Julia paused, staring at the pale, dark-shadowed reflection in the glass, trying to sort out real from imagined terror. Absurd, in morning light, to have let herself think that last night's attackers had anything to do with her search for Dominic. As Tarn had said, it must have been just a random mugging. She shivered, wondering what would have happened if that blessed water taxi had not come by. And that, though lucky, was logical enough. The deserted pier of Santa Maria Zobenigo was the kind of place

where people would be glad to settle for a taxi, however expensive. And with cause, she thought, remembering poor Tarn with his bleeding nose and his fury at
having been bested.

If only he could come with her today, as they had
originally planned. Perhaps, after all, he would telephone to say he had managed to get hold of his author
and put him off. And—perhaps not. There had been
odd undertones to last night's dinner, and, remembering them, she found herself wondering again whether
Tarn had not perhaps tired of her and her problems.
If so: hardly surprising. She made a face at her pallid
other self in the glass. Was she letting herself turn into
a bore, the kind of woman who talks forever about her
own troubles? She thought that it was when she had
spoken of Breckon that she had begun to lose touch
with Tarn. Hardly surprising. And then, suddenly
yielding to an old temptation, she pulled Breckon's
photograph out from the back of her jewel case. It
could still move her to an almost intolerable sadness.
We were right for each other, she thought. And then,
again: it was my fault. Why had she realised this so
clearly when she was talking to Tarn the night before?
Having escaped, at seventeen, from her own unloved
and unloving family, she had totally failed to understand Breckon's commitment to his.

How could he walk out on them, as she had de-
manded, straight after that disastrous fire? No one
else in the family was capable of dealing with the
sheer business involved. He had explained it to her,
patiently, at the Fort Sumter Hotel to which she had
retreated after seeing Nurse Morris into hospital.
"They're my duty, Julia, don't you see? If I abandoned

them, I might as easily abandon you." And, "But that's what you are doing," she answered.

True in a way. She had stayed for a wretched month at the hotel, while the police decided that the fire had been a mere accident, and Nurse Morris was reprimanded for sleeping on duty. She had paid Julia a furious visit. "You can speak up for me, Mrs. Rivers. You know as well as I do that was no accident. Neither the tramp, nor the fire. Just because it's the Rivers it's all to be hushed up, and I lose my chance of promotion."

"Oh, I am so sorry. But I *have* spoken," said Julia wearily. "Over and over again. To my husband. And to the police. They don't believe me. I'm an outsider."

"And I'm black." They exchanged a glance of total sympathy.

"But, surely"—Julia had been thinking about it—"at the hospital that night. They must have tested you for drugs. I told the ambulance men."

"That's queer. They certainly never did. I was put to bed and left to sleep it off, nice and quiet. Lucky for me I survived. But"—she spoke with professional fairness—"things were a shambles at St. Helen's that night, what with that highway disaster and then your fire. The ambulance men had been rushed off their feet all evening."

"St. Helen's?" It gave Julia an odd qualm. "So it was. I remember now, I'd taken it for granted we were going to the General."

"St. Helen's was nearest," said Nurse Morris. "I was lucky they took me in."

"I wonder." It was odd to have forgotten her instinctive recoil when the ambulance stopped outside the hospital, and her relief at seeing a taxi pull up behind it and discharge its passenger. At the time, she had merely felt exhausted, and thought of the comfort of a hotel rather than a hospital bed. Now she could not help remembering the confusion that had surrounded her own previous admission to St. Helen's. "Tell me," she asked, surprising herself. "Do you ever give anaesthetics for a miscarriage?"

"Not a simple one," said Nurse Morris, rising to her feet. "Well, Mrs. Rivers, there it is. You're an hysteric and I'm a nurse who sleeps on duty. I expect we'll live it down. And, by the way, thanks a million for saving my life."

"An hysteric." It should have warned her. That was what everyone was saying. No wonder if Breckon believed it. Besides, ruefully, she remembered that she had acted the part with him often enough. Not much use, now, all this time later, to tell herself that she had had some grounds for hysteria. Poor Breckon, torn between an hysterical wife and two scatty sisters. Not to mention Uncle Paul having tantrums and Raoul on the bottle.

A tear dropped on Breckon's picture and she wiped it away with her handkerchief. She put the picture away and pulled herself together to start on her day. She had lost Breckon, once, when she gave him her ultimatum after that horrible month at the hotel, and again, finally, that disastrous morning in her London flat, when she let him see she had suspected him.

All over . . . all done with—and best forgotten. Let the past be the past. How gladly she would if only she could find Dominic. What would she do if she failed? Not go back to Sir Charles. And not yield to the temptation of those hoarded sleeping pills either. Odd to find that both these decisions had made themselves in the night. She had a debt to pay. If not to Dominic, then to other children like him. Surely, somewhere, there must be a place for her, working with them . . . for them?

No message this morning. She had almost given up hoping for one. Tarn, telephoning, said angrily that he had a black eye and had failed to get hold of Mr. Heyward. "I'll have to meet him. For God's sake, be careful today, girl. Keep away from dark corners, go sightseeing, stay with the crowds. Tomorrow, we'll get to work."

"Thanks." But they must have known she would not obey him. Or not entirely. Where could she be safer than on the crowded *vaporetti?* Besides, it was all nonsense. The attack *had* to have been a random one. Putting it resolutely out of her mind, she bought her ticket at the Academia stop and decided to start the morning with the left bank. The first stage produced nothing, but the second one presented her with a problem. She passed the new cut, where the Linea Two boats turned off for the express route to the station. If she failed on the Grand Canal, she would try that. It looked wide enough, but surely too modern for the railings in Dominic's picture.

It was a long, frustrating morning, and, holding her own on her chosen side of each *vaporetto* as she went to and fro, Julia began to think she hated people. Push chairs barked her ankles; suitcases banged her back; a rucksack wielded by an immense German nearly put out her eye. And it all took so long. Down to San Toma on the left side. Back to the Academia on the other. It was twelve o'clock already. But she could do four stops next time; the two she had already done both ways, and then two more, taking her within one stop of the Rialto Bridge, where Tarn's hotel was, and, by her reckoning, about halfway down the Grand Canal.

Pushing her way with the crowd off the boat, she heard all the clocks of Venice striking twelve, and saw that the man from the ticket office had emerged with a blackboard, which he leaned up against his window before sauntering away in the direction of the café where she had lunched the day before. The message on the board was short and far from sweet. The service was suspended for two hours because of a lightning strike by the attendants.

Two hours. God, what a waste. She looked up the Academia in her guidebook, saw that it was open until one, and went in to confirm her suspicion that Tintoretto was a great bore. Then, nothing for it but to kill time over a pizza and a glass of wine in the café where, thank goodness, there were no Miss Browns today. Back sharp at two at the ferry stop, she joined the crowd that awaited the first boat, and just managed to push her way on board. For the first two stops, which she had investigated the day before, she let herself simply enjoy the small details of living along the canal, particularly the contrast between venerable palazzos that had been let go to romantic rack and ruin, and others, presumably bought and done up by big business, that sported elegant, restrained bits of bunting to advertise their wares. Then, at San Angelo, she moved over to the left-hand side of the boat and began to pay attention again. Aside from her first, exhausted trip up from the station, this was new ground—or rather new water. The boat was taking a long sweep across the canal, very wide here, towards the next stop, which her map showed on the left bank. She stiffened suddenly, trod on a high-heeled ankle, was sworn at, and took no notice. Ahead, on the left, trees leaned out over a dark railing.

Someone tried to push past her to the side, and she took hold of the rail with both hands, muttering a furious "*Prego*" over her shoulder. The railing looked right. The garden behind looked possible. And—the glimpse had been so quick she could not be sure—but something brightly coloured. A child's toy? A swing? A slide? A boy's? Dominic's?

She got off the boat at San Silvestro, actually shaking with excitement. The stop was on a wide *fondamenta*, with, farther down, an outbreak of café tables, but she turned back the way the boat had come, and pushed through loitering crowds until she reached the blank wall that ended the pavement. No way from here into the garden she had seen. She looked at her map, retraced her steps, and took the first, narrow, left turn. Left again. Now she must be almost directly behind the garden. And here, set in the high wall, was one of those elegant, characteristic, blank Venetian doors. A letterbox; a number; no name. But, high up on the right, an old-fashioned bell push. Tarn had said she must wait for him if she found anything. Ridiculous. How could she wait? She knew now that, in her heart, she had never meant to.

Firmly pulled, the bell jangled somewhere inside the house. Standing there, in the empty lane, Julia had the strangest, most unpleasant feeling of being under observation. She turned, quickly, and a curtain, on the second floor of the house across the way, fell gently back into place. It might mean anything. An old person, perhaps, with nothing to do but look out of the window? Anyway, the sound of footsteps behind that blank, black door drew all her attention. What in the world was she going to say?

A maid, very neat, very smart, in black and white, opened the door and looked at her enquiringly. For a moment, her mind was a complete blank. Then, "There is a child here?" she asked, in her fluent Italian.

"*Si*, signora?" The girl made it a question.

Julia took a firm step into the tiled hall and looked about her. Everything she saw spelt money, well spent. The whole interior of the palazzo must have been gutted and replaced in a plain modern style that pleased her. She took another step forward, recognizing a picture on the wall as one of Grandma Moses' primitives. "May I speak to the lady of the house?" She managed a calm confidence she was very far from feeling.

"The lady?" The girl looked puzzled. "But there is no lady. Only the signor."

"Oh." How strange. "Then, if I might see him?" She took another tentative step forward towards the big balustraded central stair that led up to the main floor.

Now the girl was barring her way, politely, but with some firmness. "I must first ask," she said. "The signora's name?"

"Mrs. Rivers." Julia saw a flicker of something— amazement?—cross the sallow face.

"I will tell the signor." The girl gestured to an

antique settle that stood against one wall of the big, cool entrance hall.

"Thank you." Julia shook her head and moved over to look at the lively little picture of flowers and children as the girl ran up and round the corner of the stairs. How would one get out to the garden? Doors on each side of the stairway, at the back of the hall, must lead to it, by the way, probably, of the servants' quarters. But her situation was odd enough as it was. She turned away from those tempting doors to take a quick inventory of her own appearance in a huge looking glass that hung to the right of the entrance. Yes, she would pass muster in this elegant house. Sir Charles had taught her well. The dark, cool-looking figure in the glass might have stepped out of *Vogue*. Inside, somewhere, cowered the slum child, and all the nameless faces and fears that haunted her. Outside, all looked well with her. How strange it was. . . .

She pulled fresh white gloves out of her bag and turned to meet the maid, who was coming downstairs, looking, surely, flustered.

"He says you are to come up, signora."

"Thank you." Following the girl up shallow stairs, Julia thought that something had shaken her badly. For the first time, she wished, passionately, that she had not followed impulse and come alone. She should have waited for Tarn.

The upper hall was tiled like the one below, but narrower. The maid opened a big door and ushered Julia into a room full of light. Huge windows along the canal side of the palazzo had their shutters thrown back to let in morning sunshine, which was reflected, dazzlingly, by a mirror-wall on either side of the doorway. A man, standing to receive her, was, for a moment, only a silhouette against the light.

Behind her, the door shut softly on the maid. Julia took a hesitant step forward. "My apologies for this intrusion," she began in Italian, and then, "Dear God, Breckon!"

"So it is you. 'Mrs. Rivers.' I trust you don't expect a welcome."

"But—I don't understand." It was true. She understood nothing, and, least of all, what had happened to Breckon. No wonder she had not recognised him in silhouette against the light. Where was the dark-suited, formal young man she had married? This stranger had fair, well-brushed curling hair down to his shoulders and wore a scarlet silk shirt with narrow black corduroys. Only the face, looking at her with something beyond dislike, had not changed, except that she had never seen him look so brown and healthy, and surely, impossibly, younger?

"Why should you understand?" He placed a chair for her with its back to the window. "And, more important, why the hell are you here? A little late, surely, for that?"

"You mean—" It was extraordinary: at once too good to be true, and too painful to be borne. "You have got him? Dominic?"

"My son. Yes. No thanks to you." And then, "How in God's name do you know his name?"

"I had a letter." Ignoring the chair, she moved towards the window. "Breckon, please, may I see him?"

"I can hardly stop you looking out of the window. But if you mean, talk to him: no. You lost that right when you abandoned him. We've come a long way, he and I. You're not going to spoil it now. I told him you were dead. It seemed . . . kindest."

It was salt in the old wound, but she was absorbed in gazing down out of the wide window at the garden, with its small grass-plot, its fringe of trees, and all that apparatus for happy childhood. It was probably the brightly coloured, child-sized slide that had caught her attention from the canal. And, there, at the top, sat a fair-haired boy, his good hand held by a dark, beautiful, smiling girl, who now, gently, pushed him off to zoom down the slide, exploding with happy laughter as he went.

"How could you?" asked Breckon. And then, "No, I don't want to know. It's enough that you did."

"Yes." She looked up at him with tear-drowned eyes. "You're right. Only—I was ill, Breckon. I didn't know what to do."

"It didn't occur to you to get in touch with me? I am, after all, his father. That's obvious enough, poor little bastard." They stood together, in an odd appearance of amity, looking down at their child, who was now making skilful use of his left arm to help his right one as he climbed back up the ladder to the top of the slide.

"He's wonderfully better," she said.

"Of course he is! If you knew what he's been through. But that's no affair of yours."

"Breckon! I meant to write to you. After he was born." The words came painfully. "Only, when he was like that. . . . After what you said, that last morning, how could I? Besides"—she was trying to be honest with herself as well as with him—"I suppose, in a way it was an excuse. I didn't want to, you see. Get in touch with you. I didn't think it was any of your business. After you didn't answer my letters. After . . . oh, after all of it. And, of course, before he was born, I thought I could manage. On my own. Only—I was ill, afterwards. That's another reason I didn't write. By the time I was strong enough, it seemed too late. The lawyer said—" She was blushing, horribly, painfully, remembering how gently Sir Charles' young lawyer had broken it to her. "Dominic was born late," she explained. "Three weeks. He said—the lawyer—you might not believe. . . . And the doctors said I couldn't cope on my own. He needed so much. So—" She would not tell this angry stranger about the breakdown that had followed her decision. But, "It was you all along?" she asked. "You adopted him?"

"My son."

"How did you know?"

"No thanks to you. By sheer good luck. I was passing through London, on my way here. I"—just for a moment his expression softened—"I remembered what I'd said that morning, too. I wanted to make sure you were all right. Maybe had found someone else. . . . So I called your office and was told you were in the hospital. After that, it was simple."

"You didn't come to see me."

"Why should I? You hadn't told me." It was unanswerable.

"And you've had him ever since?"

"Well, of course."

"And knew I was looking for him, and didn't tell me." In so much that was unbearable, this was the worst.

"No. How should I know you were looking for him?

I left instructions, at the start, that there must be no back trail. Theoretically, mind you, there never is, but I made extra sure."

"You certainly did. But——" She was completely in a fog, and found herself, oddly, remembering that morning, back at Charleston, when only river mist had saved her. "Breckon, what are you doing here? I don't understand anything. . . ."

"Why should you?" But, now, curiously, he sounded defensive. "In a way," he said with an effort, "I suppose I owe you an apology, Julia."

"Oh?" Below them, in the garden, the child had grown tired of the slide, and he and his dark-haired companion had moved over, hand in hand, to the small swing that hung from an ilex. And, below them in the house, the doorbell jangled.

"You were right about La Rivière," he said. "Something very queer *was* going on there. I—decided to come away."

"Breckon, why? What happened?"

"Why should I tell you?"

"I—don't know." She spoke the words slowly, fighting tears.

"My family," he said, and then, in Italian, "Yes, Maria?"

"There are two ladies." She handed him a letter. "They ask to see you."

"Excuse me?" Formally, to Julia, who suspected him of being relieved at the interruption. He opened the letter and read it with his old quick concentration. "I'll have to see them," he said. "Friends of the girls. Leaving tonight. Besides, we've said all there is."

"*No!*" She had not thought she could be so angry.

"How can you say that? I want to see my child, Breckon. I *mean* to see him. Besides, there's more." She must tell him about the anonymous letters.

"You are not going to see the child." The carefully spaced words carried their own sense of finality, and Julia saw the maid flash him a puzzled glance for their tone. He turned to her. "Show the ladies up." And then, in face of Julia's impending outburst, "I have to see them. Give me the name of your hotel. I'll ring you—Not tonight. I'm busy. Tomorrow. Anything you want to say, say then. And then, that's all."

"You're cruel!" Tears blinded her and she turned away from the window, through which she could no longer see.

"As cruel as you were when you abandoned him?" And then, once again with evident relief, he turned to the door, where Maria was ushering in—the Miss Browns.

"Mr. Rivers." The expression of the elder of the two showed that she was aware of the quarrel they had interrupted. "How good of you to see us." And then, as her eyes grew accustomed to the dazzling light of the room, "Good gracious, and *Mrs*. Rivers?" The question hung, half-spoken in the air.

It got no answer. "How do you do." Breckon shook the two outstretched hands. And then, inevitably, "You know Mrs. Rivers?"

"We met on the train," the elder Miss Brown explained.

"A small place, Venice," said her sister.

"We've all kinds of messages for you from the girls," said Miss Brown. "And one from Dr. McCartland. Rather—well, rather confidential, I'm afraid.

He said it was a mercy we were coming."

I'm going crazy, thought Julia. How could she have failed to notice that faint, unmistakable American accent?

"We've been back home for a visit." This was the younger Miss Brown. "Then just a night back in London and straight here. Dr. McCartland said it was better than writing. We called yesterday." She anticipated a question that had just asked itself in Julia's mind. "But nobody answered. And now, what luck to have found you. We're off to Florence in the morning. We've a million things still to see here, but a reservation's a reservation, isn't it?"

"Yes, indeed." Breckon pulled forward chairs for them. "I mustn't waste your valuable time. If you'll excuse us?" There was to be no chair for Julia. "Maria!" He raised his voice. "The signora is leaving." And, to Julia, "I'll ring you tomorrow."

It was final, and she knew it. "Very well. The Da Rimini. Good-bye." She had swallowed her tears, painfully, by now, and managed civil farewells to the Miss Browns.

"Don't forget the Academia," said the elder, as Maria appeared in the doorway.

"I won't." Following the maid down the wide stairway, Julia suddenly realised that now she had all the time in the world to sightsee. She had found Dominic, and found him lost beyond recall.

The big door shut quietly behind her. She would not accept it. In the end, surely, Breckon would understand. There had been a moment, back there, when he was talking about La Rivière, when she had thought things were opening up again, just a little, between them. If only the Miss Browns had not arrived. Odd about the Miss Browns. . . . The alley was cool, shadowed, and empty. Automatically, she made a note of its name, and the number of Breckon's house, wishing all the time she had told him about the letters that had brought her here. For some reason, the discovery that Dominic was well, happy, and in the best possible hands—except her own—had made them seem more rather than less sinister. Almost, she rang the bell and insisted on returning. But it would not work, and she knew it. She would hurry back to the Da Rimini and telephone from there. She hailed a water taxi and was back at the hotel in ten minutes.

But there was no Rivers in the telephone book, and the operator disclaimed all knowledge of such a number. What then? A note, of course. She would write at once and take it back with her. More and more, a sense of urgency drove her. She was turning away from that exposed telephone at the desk, when Tarn Menzies' voice stopped her. "Julia!" He had just come in from the street. "My oath, here's luck. I ditched Mr. Heyward and came by on the off-chance. My God, girl, I think I've found it. Where's that picture, so we can check?" And then, looking round the lobby, and, belatedly, remembering the need for caution. "Come and have a coffee?"

"Love to." He was just what she needed after that brutal reception from Breckon. "I'll be with you in a moment." She turned back to the desk and asked the girl there for an envelope. Then, rejoining Tarn, "I found it, too," she said quietly, as he held the door for her.

"You did?" And then, "Sure. What a fool I am. You

were bound to. Just above the Rialto? I spotted it this
morning when I took Heyward to the Ca' Rezzonica.
Can't think why I didn't sooner. Looking the other way;
that's the strength of it. But—you think it's right?"
They had reached a small cafè tucked away in a minor
square between the Da Rimini and the Salute, and he
pulled out a hard chair for her and ordered two
espresssos from an idling waiter.

"I know it's right. I've been there." She tried not
to look at his black eye and swollen cheek.

"You've been? But you promised, girl! Thank God,
you seem to have got away all right, but don't you
see, you've blown the game. They're likely moving
him right now." He pushed back his chair. "We'd
better go straight over."

"No need," she said. "It's not what we thought at all.
My husband's got him."

"Your husband!"

"My ex-husband." She corrected it wearily. "He's
had him all the time."

"I thought he didn't know?"

"So did I. Apparently he came to London when I
was in hospital and found out . . . all about it. He's
had Dominic ever since." It reminded her of the urgency
of the situation. "But, Tarn, what am I to do? He didn't
give me a chance to tell him about the letters, I was
going to, but some people came. He practically threw
me out."

"Tough." Tarn's sympathy was balm. "But, one
thing—you know the child's OK. Did you see him?"

"Not to speak to. Breckon wouldn't let me. Just out
the window. He looks fine."

"Well, there you are. Drink your coffee, there's a girl;

you look like three cents' worth of God help us."

She sipped obediently at the black brew. "Tarn, I'm so worried. Nothing seems to make sense. I mean, Breckon's got Dominic. Everything's fine. Not for me, of course, but for Dominic, which is what matters. But—what about the letters? Where do they fit in?"

"Someone trying to make trouble between you and your ex," said Tarn at once. "Sounds like that family of his to me. Suppose they've got the idea the kid's more than just adopted, mightn't they be afraid it might mean a makeup between you two?"

"But then, why bring me out here?"

"Queer as Dick's hatband. But, then, they sure sound a ropey lot. Maybe they've laid the ground somehow, so you and your husband are bound to quarrel."

"They didn't need to," she said bitterly. "I think he hates me already."

"They weren't to know that. And, come to think, what's he doing all this way from home? I thought he was fixed for life at that place—what d'you call it?— La Rivière."

"So did I. That was odd, too. He said something about owing me an apology. I think he'd got on to it that something really was wrong there. Only then the Miss Browns came."

He gave a long, soundless whistle. "The Miss Browns? The ones from the train? What the hell were they doing there?"

"Wasn't it odd? It turns out they're from Charleston really, just living in England. They'd been back there, and brought a message for Breckon, they said, from Dr. McCartland. It's extraordinary. I can't think how I missed the accent before."

"For a bet, because they weren't using it. Come on, girl, use your head. The Miss Browns sound like your answer."

"What do you mean?"

"For a start: what was the message?"

"I don't know. They said it was private. That was when Breckon threw me out."

"And now they're busy as bandicoots poisoning his mind against you. Tough. If you'd only got there half an hour earlier. . . ."

"But what do I do now?"

"Play it slow and cool. Of course"—was there a mocking sparkle in his dark eyes?—"first you need to make up that mind of yours just what you *do* want. Maybe the old folks at home have got it right. Maybe you are burning the midnight for that stuffed-shirt husband of yours. Maybe you do want to give him another chance to let you down, like always. Take you back to La Rivière and get you hit over the head again. Maybe for keeps, this time. But even if that is what you want"—he silenced her with a hand—"I still say you should play it cool and slow. They think you'll panic: start telephoning, writing, generally get in his hair. Right?" He looked at his watch. "So, instead you come out to Torcello with me, forget your troubles, and give him time to think things over. He can't be a complete fool or you wouldn't have married him. So—give him time. Time to get his cool back and realise he has to let you see the child. If that's what you really care about."

"Of course it is."

"Well, there you are." He snapped his fingers for the bill. "Let's go. My oath, those Miss Browns will probably overplay the hand anyway. They sound like a proper pair of amateurs to me. Imagine letting their accents slip. A bright girl like you was bound to spot it. Look how you spotted mine. I don't think you need lose much hair over them. Chances are that husband of yours is having second thoughts already. He knows where he can find you?"

"Oh, yes. He said he'd call me tomorrow, at the Da Rimini."

"Goodoh. There you are. Don't call him. Let him call you." He paid and tipped the waiter. "Much better that way, and you know it, girl. Come on, let's go. We'll have to shake a leg if we're going to get that boat."

There was something wonderfully reassuring about his calm commonsense. She had been letting herself get into what Breckon would have called "one of her states," and Tarn was right, nothing could have been more fatal. Glad to have the burden of decision lifted from her, she let him take her arm and guide her down to the canal by the Salute where water taxis often waited.

"We'll just make it, with a bit of 'Strine's luck." He helped her in and spoke rapidly, in Italian, to the boatman, who also consulted his watch, then nodded. Yes, they could indeed cut across the main island to the north shore and just catch the Torcello boat.

In fact, they were held up by a water ambulance, siren screaming, on its way to the Civil Hospital, and ended by running down the new quay and panting, last on board, onto the Linea Twelve boat that went to Murano, Burano, and Torcello. Tarn led the way to the top deck, which was blessedly uncrowded this late in the afternoon. "Here." He settled them in two seats, looking forward and to the right. "We won't have long on Torcello, but the ride will do you good."

"How long does it take?" Now that the boat had started she was riven by second thoughts. Tarn might well be right in his analysis of her situation, but suppose he was not? Suppose there was something more sinister about that series of letters than mere family jealousy, and she had failed to warn Breckon? Now, she knew she should have written that note. Calmly and coolly, perhaps, but written it, at least, and dropped it in to that elegant house of his. She would do it the minute she got back.

"Only an hour." Tarn's cheerful answer took her breath away.

"An hour!" Concentrating on the main islands, she had no idea Torcello was so far away.

"Relax, Scheherazade. You're on holiday now, remember? Day off. Look, there's the cemetery island."

"A whole island?" She looked in amazement at the walled island, with its cypresses dark against the blue of the sky.

"Tidier that way. Not bad to be buried there. With a full-blast gondola funeral."

She was hardly listening. She could see what must be the island of Murano ahead and was trying to decide how to break it to him that she must go back and write her note to Breckon. The farther they got from Venice, the more her sense of urgency grew. She would make Tarn understand. But he had risen, with a quick apology, and left her. And now, the lighthouse on Murano was straight ahead, the boat was slowing down and swinging in to the dock. For a moment, she seriously considered abandoning Tarn, but how could she, after all the help he had given her?

He did not reappear until the boat was well out into the posted channel across the lagoon. "Dirty big queue." He sat down beside her.

"Pity." Her voice came out dry. "I'd been meaning to suggest we go back from Murano. I'm sorry, Tarn, but I think I owe it to Breckon to tell him about those letters. As soon as possible. Do you mind if we get off at Burano?"

"No use, girl. We'd have to wait for the same boat back as if we'd gone on to Torcello. Stop making mountains out of molehills. You've found the child. Right? He's OK. Right? So—relax. You don't want to give that ex-husband of yours the idea that you're after *him*. Fatal. Eh? Specially if there's any chance of another woman in the picture. What was that you said about a stunning Sheila playing with young Dominic? Don't you see, girl, the strength of it is that you don't give a damn about Breckon, but will fight him till the cows come home for the right to see your child. For God's sake don't muck it all up now. Write him a note, if you like, when we get back. Or in the café on Torcello. Show him you've got your own life; date it Torcello." He laughed. "Say you're on a date. He's much more likely to play along. I'll drop it in on my way home tonight. Make a point of being seen, if you like. Or we both could. Look!" He broke off to point across the boat. "Look at the mountains!"

They hung, like a cloud, like a mirage, far off to the north, with the sun picking out snow on their peaks. "They're beautiful." Tarn was right, Julia thought.

The situation between her and Breckon was difficult enough without her rushing into the kind of impulsive action he had always disliked. But then, an odd thought. What did she know about the new Breckon, the one who wore long hair and scarlet shirts? Maybe he liked impulsive action now. And maybe not. Her note to him would need careful drafting. With possible phrases drifting about at the back of her mind, she paid civil attention as Tarn pointed out the posts that marked the channel, with their electric lights for guidance at night, and notices that prohibited anchoring or shellfishing.

"What a ravishing place." She was gazing ahead at a low island, with walls, a few dilapidated buildings, and a wild, green tangle of undergrowth.

"Deserted now," he told her. "Some kind of military installation in the war. There are lots more like it, dotted about the lagoon. Not at all deserted. Pretty fancy living on some of them. See!" A speedboat had come roaring towards the main channel from a farther cypress-crowned island.

Julia looked at her watch. "I wish we'd get there," she said.

Eight

THAT AFTERNOON at Torcello was a nightmare of its own. To begin with, the island, with its lush, neglected green growth of vegetable garden and vineyard reminded Julia in a strange, disconcerting way of La Rivière. And from La Rivière to Breckon and Dominic was just one agonizing mind's breath. She ought to have told Breckon about the anonymous letters. It seemed incredible, now, in retrospect, to have let herself be brushed aside so easily. And—again—should she have let Tarn persuade (over-persuade?)

her to this afternoon's outing.

Stopping beside him on the path to pretend to admire the village green, with its scatter of grey buildings and huge, dominating cathedral and bell tower, she paid them only token attention. "Tarn, what am I going to do?"

"Quit worrying, for Christ's sake!" He had never used that tone with her before and must have seen her face change. "Sorry, girl, I'm as low as hell myself today. And work to do before I face Mr. Author Heyward again. So, you run along, relax, enjoy yourself. I'll be right here, nose to the grindstone."

"Oh!" Stupid of her not to have realised that for Tarn, inevitably this must be partly—mainly?—a business trip. It had been his own necessity that had made him take such a firm line with her doubts. Mad to have come. And nothing, now, that she could do about it. As he settled down to one of his rather scratchy line drawings of the cathedral's towering façade, she moved reluctantly towards it.

"That's right," said Tarn more cheerfully. "Go say hullo to the Madonna for me. She's worth it."

Disconcerting, as always, to have to pay to go into a church. But, once inside, Julia stopped dead at sight of the huge, tragic, triumphant figure that dominated the main aisle. She stumbled to a chair and sat, her knees weak. How could the mosaic workers who had built up the great portrait have come so deep to the quick of a mother's grief? She found she was both praying and crying, but quietly, not to disturb the great silence of the church.

It was disturbed, after a while, by a crowd of tourists who must have come on one of the special excursions to the island, and she rose to flee from their exclamations and flashlit cameras. "Super, isn't it?" The girl's accent stopped her at the main door, and she recognised the young couple she had met the day before.

"Even my barbarian likes it." The tall young man, Peter, had recognised Julia, too. But, "Come on, Sue you get the best view from the bottom of the aisle. Be seeing you," he dismissed Julia.

Outside, she forgot them at once. Tarn had disappeared. Absurd not to have remembered how quickly he did those sketches of his. But he could not be far off. She walked quickly around the corner of the cathedral, saw no sign of him, and retraced her steps to investigate the open gallery of the small, incredibly ancient-looking baptistry. But its door was firmly shut, and the priest who took the money at the cathedral door shook his head at her. Tarn could not possibly be inside.

To make bad worse, the sky was darkening. She looked at her watch. She had sat longer in the cathedral than she thought. Only twenty minutes now until the Venice boat was due, and the walk to the jetty took nearly ten. They ought to go soon, especially if it was going to rain. She started round the cathedral in the other direction and found herself involved in a series of marsh paths that again reminded her painfully of La Rivière. From somewhere ahead, a siren sounded. The excursion boat must be moored on this side of the island. "Hi there!" Peter and Sue came running down the path. "It's going to pour. D'you want a lift back?"

"Could I?" The temptation was irresistible.

"Sure." Again it was Peter who spoke. "The guide's

a friend of mine, and it's not full. You'll be drowned by the time you get to the regular stop." Huge drops of rain were beginning to fall.

"Yes." She hesitated. "But—I'm with someone." As she spoke, she heard Tarn's voice calling her.

"Julia!" He appeared, breathless, round the end of the cathedral. "Where the hell have you been?"

"Looking for you." She did not try to keep the reproach out of her voice.

"For me? But I came into the cathedral for you, soon as I saw the storm coming. You'd slung off."

"Oh, how maddening!" It was the one thing she had not thought of. "We must have just missed each other."

He looked at his watch. "Too late for the boat now. We'll have to sit out the storm in the café."

"Well. . . ." She looked hopefully at their two young companions.

"Yes, of course," said Peter. "Wouldn't leave a dog out in weather like this. Come on—" The siren sounded again. "*Direttissimo*." He led the way swiftly across a bridge and down a path to where the excursion boat was moored in a deep channel.

It was smaller than Julia had expected, but there was just room for everyone under cover. No room, though, for writing her note to Breckon, and not much time to plan it, with tourist talk flashing this way and that, like the lightning overhead. But at least the ride back—*direttissimo* as Peter had said—was blessedly quick, and landed them at St. Mark's instead of at the Linea Twelve stop on the north side of the island. It was still pouring with rain, but Julia refused to stop and shelter over a drink. She half expected Tarn to escort her back to the Da Rimini, but he explained, with a touch of apology, that he had arranged to dine with his author. "I'll ring you in the morning." A quick glance at his watch. "Sorry, girl, I said I'd drop your note in, didn't I? Thought you'd get it written out at Torcello. Trouble is, now, by the time you've got it done. . . . I can't be late for Mr. Dammit Heyward. Besides, I bet your sweet life you're going to find a message from your Breckon back at the hotel. Full of humble pie."

"I do hope so." She saw her boat coming and ran for it through drenching rain.

By the time she got to the Da Rimini her hair was in dripping rats' tails on her neck, and water sogged in her shoes. The lobby was crowded with refugees from the rain, and she was working her way towards the desk when a cold hand fell on hers. "What have you done with him?" asked Breckon in a voice she hardly recognised.

"Done? What do you mean? What's the matter?" He, too, had been out in the rain and his fair hair clung close to his skull, but that was not what gave the death's-head look to his face.

"Come here." He pulled her, not gently, into a small room that was kept unlighted by the frugal management of the hotel. Then, turning her face to the drowned light from the window: "Don't pretend not to understand. Just tell me what you've done with him, and that he's not been too frightened, and maybe, in a million years, I'll think of forgiving you."

Her teeth were chattering. "Breckon! Dominic? You don't mean—"

"Don't hedge. You know just what I mean. Didn't

take you long, did it? You had it all arranged, I suppose? Brought a posse of some kind along with you? Friends of Sir Charles'? Even now, even after everything—I wouldn't have believed it of you."

"And you'd have been right." Horror and anger, evenly balanced, almost choked her. "Breckon, you've got to *tell* me. Dominic's been——"

"Kidnapped. As if I had to tell you! But maybe Sir Charles didn't explain all his delightful plans for my son. If you must have it spelled out, here you are. He went to the beach—the Lido—this afternoon, with Lucia, his nurse. When the rain started, they ran for the *vaporetto*, with a million other people. They were holding hands, she says. Laughing together in the rain. Suddenly his face changed. 'Lucy,' he said. He speaks English, mostly, 'I don't feel——' And then, he was pulled one way and she the other, and he was gone. Not a scream, not a sound. She thinks he must have been drugged, right there in the crowd, and just carried away. Easy enough, a little boy like him." He was watching her face with a kind of furious intensity as he 'talked, and now gave a sigh of angry satisfaction. "You didn't expect that, did you?"

"Breckon, you've got to believe me. I didn't expect any of this." It was more horrible than the worst of her fears, but at all costs she must keep her head, and convince Breckon, against the odds, that he and she were on the same side—Dominic's.

"No? You thought it would be all sweetness and light? Sir Charles driving up in a flowery chariot and carrying off my son to realms of glory? That kind of thing? Nothing so vulgar as drugs and kidnapping. And where is he now? Dominic. He's afraid of the dark. He doesn't admit it, but I know. So—where is he?"

"Breckon, I don't know." Idiotic never to have realised that he was jealous of Sir Charles. And, simply, now, another huge block in the wall of misunderstanding between them. Of which nothing mattered but Dominic and his danger. And that was so horribly worse than Breckon had realised. "Please." She held out a desperate cold hand to him. "You must listen. Try to understand. You wouldn't this afternoon. I don't blame you. But, now, for Dominic's sake, you must."

"Let it get out of hand have you?" A quick, impatient glance at his watch. "Ten minutes to go. I promised Lucia that if you weren't here, or didn't make sense, I'd telephone the police at five sharp."

"You haven't yet?"

Now, for the first time, the horror in her voice carried its own conviction. His face changed. "You can't mean . . . Julia, you haven't got him? I was so sure. . . ."

"I can't blame you. And it's all my fault, in a way." Could he possibly have delayed calling in the police for her sake? But a mistake just the same. Perhaps a disastrous one.

"Of course it's your fault." Inevitably, he took it wrong. "I'm glad at least you have the grace to admit it. I suppose you just didn't let yourself think how Sir Charles would set about it. Well, you know now. And I'll put the police on to *you*, Julia, if I don't have him back tonight."

"But I haven't *got* him," she waited. "That's what I'm trying to tell you, Breckon, only you won't listen, just the way you wouldn't this morning. Yes?" She turned impatiently as the girl from the desk entered the room.

"Telephone for you, Signora."

The kidnappers? "Coming." She turned back to Breckon. "Perhaps it's them. The people who've got him. They wrote me anonymous letters. That's why I'm here. That's what I tried to tell you. Why I'm so frightened. Breckon, go to the police at once. No, wait, now, just in case it is them——" She hurried after the girl into the crowded lobby and picked up the receiver on the desk. "Yes?"

"Signora Rivers?" It was an unknown, Italian voice, and hope surged in her.

"Yes," she said again, breathlessly.

"Good. There is someone wishes to speak to you. One moment please, signora. I will put you through." The telephone went silent, as if a line had been plugged in at a switchboard.

"Hullo?" said Julia into the silence. No answer, just the odd, crackling noises of a connected telephone. "Hullo?" Her voice rose as she repeated it, and instinctively, she looked at her watch. Five o'clock. The time when Breckon had promised to go to the police. Promised Lucia. What was the relation between them? Something Tarn had said. . . . Shameful to be thinking of this, now, with Dominic in what she felt to be horrible danger. And yet—why? Almost, she found herself hoping that this was merely an ordinary kidnapping, of which, God knew, one heard often enough. But, if so, why the anonymous letters? "Hullo!" she said again into the silent telephone and, looking across the crowded hotel lobby, saw Breckon emerge from the little room, a piece of paper in his hand, and push his way through the crowd to the street door. He must have heard from them. She longed to run after him, but must not. The telephone she held, as easily as the note he had got, might be a lifeline to Dominic.

The girl at the desk was looking at her impatiently. "You have finished, signora?"

"No, I don't seem to have got through yet. Hullo?" Her voice lacked conviction, even to her. A quick glance at her watch showed that almost five minutes had ebbed away. An English girl was standing beside her, waiting to use the telephone, making a poor attempt at hiding impatience.

"Let me?" The girl at the desk took the receiver, and as she did so, Julia heard the click as the line was disconnected and the dial tone resumed. "Finished." She handed the receiver to the English girl.

Useless to protest. There was no way she could persuade them to keep this telephone free in case the unknown Italian called again. She turned and pushed in her turn through the crowded lobby, trying to convince herself she was not too late to catch Breckon. But, outside, there was no sign of him. She stood for a moment, stock-still in pouring rain, wondering in anguish whether to go back and wait for another call or to follow instinct and head for Breckon's house.

Instinct won. After all, he had had that note. She was moving already, half running, in the direction of the canal and another water taxi. It took longer to get one this time, and when she did arrive, it was to an impasse. The door was opened by the Italian girl, Lucia. Her face just showed round the crack at which she held it, on the chain. When Julia asked for Breckon, she shook her head. The signor had gone out and not returned.

So the note had not brought him home. Was this good news? She had to think so. "May I come in and wait?"

"No," said the girl. "The signor said no one. I am sorry."

How much did she know? Enough to share Breckon's horrible suspicions? Very likely. It was unpleasantly easy to imagine that, even in her own distress, she was taking a certain pleasure in Julia's. "When he comes back," said Julia, "tell him I must speak to him. Ask him to telephone me. And"—thank God she had remembered—"please, may I have your telephone number?"

"There is no telephone," said the girl. "The signor does not like them."

True? False? Impossible to tell. "Well, then. Ask him, please, to come and see me. At the Hotel Da Rimini. Mrs. Rivers."

"I know." The girl closed the door.

Standing outside that blank face, Julia wished passionately, for a moment, that she had seized the momentary chance when the chain was down, and forced her way in. And yet, what purpose would it have served? She turned, aware all at once of just how cold and wet and wretched she was, and made her way fast as she could back to the Da Rimini. Perhaps there would be a telephone message. Perhaps. . . .

There was none. She knew she had not expected it and had already been planning what to do next. As usual, someone was using the telephone. She waited impatiently, then rang Tarn's hotel, only to learn he had gone out, presumably to meet his author. So, that was that. Breckon would have called in the police by now. Incredibly, there was nothing else, for the moment, that she could do. Or—was there? She asked the girl to place a call to England, gave her Sir Charles' number, and hurried upstairs, at last, to get out of her cold wet clothes. Now there really *was* nothing to do except wait, make herself eat tasteless food in the rapidly emptying dining room, and hope to God she would hear from Breckon before Sir Charles' call came through.

Nothing came through. No word from Breckon. And the girl at the desk reported, first, that the lines to England were all busy, then, incredibly, that there was no answer from Sir Charles' number. Which was always monitored. Rather sulkily, the girl rechecked the number with Julia. It was correct. She agreed, with a cross look at her watch, to try again. This time, Julia stood by the desk as she put the call through, concentrating on the quickly spoken Italian numerals. Yes, it was Sir Charles' private number, and yet, once again, when, more quickly at this time of night, the connection was made, there was no answer. "They are probably having a strike," said the girl helpfully. "And now, signora, it is time I went."

"But if a call comes through for me?"

"The night man will be here. You wish to be waked?"

"Yes, please. At any time." And yet, somehow, she did not hope to be.

Of course, the bath water was cold by now, and Julia went chilly to bed with little expectation of sleep. Lying rigid with anxiety, she thought of Dominic, who was afraid of the dark. In what dark place had they got him tonight? And why had Breckon not telephoned to tell her about the note? Surely, its very arrival must have convinced him of her innocence. Or—must it? She shivered convulsively at the thought of the wall of suspicion that had built itself between her and Breckon. Built itself? Or been built, carefully, hint by hint, stone by stone, pebble by pebble. As long ago as at La Rivière.

Now, looking back, she was sure of it. Someone, then, had been deliberately, skilfully, subtly poisoning Breckon's mind against her. And—someone he loved and trusted, or it would not, could not have worked. It was curious what a light her recognition of Breckon's jealousy of Sir Charles had cast over their whole situation. Breckon had met and worked with Sir Charles, back in Paris. A million years ago it seemed now. They had liked and respected each other, and it had been totally understood between the three of them that Sir Charles' opposition to their marriage had been, simply, because he hated to lose her. "An old man's selfishness," she remembered him saying, to both of them, giving them a lavish dinner when they announced their engagement. "You're a lucky man, Rivers, and don't you forget it."

A long time ago. Would she never be warm again? What had the unknown enemy managed to make Breckon believe about her and Sir Charles? That they were lovers? Had always been? It would make a kind of horrible sense. She suddenly thought of that secretary of Sir Charles' who had not much liked his habit of taking his assistant to lunch. Suppose someone had sent Breckon to talk to her? What would she have said?

Something, perhaps, that could have been twisted, with the help of a clever, dominating mind. Because, no doubt about it, Sir Charles had been Pygmalion to her Galatea. Only—that was *all* it was. He had recognised the possibilities of the awkward, desperate child of seventeen who had passed a written test so brilliantly that he had decided, on impulse, to see her. And he had seen through the shabby gym tunic, the wrinkled black stockings, the old blazer in which she had run away to London; seen, even, through that formidable Glaswegian accent of hers, to the person underneath. A person, he had decided on the spot, who could be useful to him.

He had put her through a ruthless training, always at one remove. The gift of total recall, and the brain, "like a computer" on which he had congratulated her, that first day, had been sharpened to razor-keenness at the extraordinary finishing school to which he had sent her. And at the same time she had learned so many other things. How to speak, how to dress, how to eat; almost, it seemed, how to live.

How had he paid the bills for all that schooling? Surely, not directly. But—if someone had managed to trace them back to him? Shown the results to Breckon? Someone Breckon trusted? She lay, fighting the old horrors, thinking of Uncle Paul, who could walk if he had a mind to . . . of Raoul, who was not always drunk . . . of gentle Fanny and kind Amanda. Fanny, who had frightened her so, that day in the hospital, when she came, unannounced, with flowers. But (she and Sir Charles had come back to this over and over again when they discussed that disastrous time) the family had all been together, that day she was attacked. And, if it had been hard, then, to believe any of them capable of contriving all that dark plot, it was impossible, now, to imagine them reaching out a hand, half across the world, to attack Breckon and her here.

And where did that leave her? In the dark, like poor little Dominic. She let herself cry, and, at last, exhausted, slept.

Morning. And no message. Nothing from Tarn, either. He must have been up late with his author. She must eat some breakfast, but after that, even if it meant she also missed a phone call, she would go back to Breckon's house and insist on seeing him. But, after breakfast, the police came.

There were two of them, very polite. The management had turned on the lights in the dark little saloon for them, and they had placed a chair for Julia under the dusty chandelier. Standing between her and the window, the door closed behind them, they established, swiftly, that she was indeed Signora Rivers and that her Italian was better than their English. Or so they said. "But what is it?" She had bitten back the question impatiently through the necessary preliminaries. "Is there news of the child?"

"Nothing. Indeed, we hoped you might have news for us, signora."

"Oh, no." She put distracted hands to her head. "But I told Signor Rivers. Surely, when he thought it over he must have realised I had nothing to do with it. The kidnapping."

"Ah." The two men let out a kind of mutual sigh. "So you admit that you saw Signor Rivers?" asked the senior of the two.

"Admit? Of course, I admit it. I told him to come to you—at once. It's fatal, isn't it, to delay over a kidnapping?"

"When did you see him?"

"Why?" Absurd to waste time with this type of question, but the quickest way of dealing with them, she knew, was to answer. She looked at her watch, thinking back. "A little before five yesterday afternoon."

"And you quarrelled." It was not a question.

"I suppose someone listening might have thought so. But what does it matter? The thing is, now he has told you about the kidnapping, what are you doing to find the child?"

"Your child, signora?"

"Yes." Hard-held patience was slipping away. "Hence my concern."

"Naturally. Only, signora, you are under a misapprehension. It was not Signor Rivers who reported the child as missing."

"No? Then how do you know?"

"Because the nursemaid telephoned us. Lucia Capella."

"Of course," said Julia with relief. "How sensible of her. At five o'clock, aş he said?"

The younger of the two policemen started to speak, but was interrupted by his superior. "Later. For the moment, signora, if you would be good enough to tell us what you and Signor Rivers discussed."

"But that's absurd," she protested. "Of course we talked about the kidnapping. He thought I had had something to do with it." The admission was incredibly painful, but Sir Charles had taught her that the truth is always the quickest. "I think I had almost convinced him that I was as appalled as he was, and that we must get in touch with you at once, when I was called to the telephone. I hoped it might be the kidnappers," she explained.

"And was it?"

"I don't know. They kept me on the line for about five minutes and then rang off. By then I had seen Breck—Signor Rivers leaving. He had a note in his hand. I thought it must be from them. I ran after him, but he'd vanished. I went to his house, but the girl, Lucia, wouldn't let me in."

"And then—"

"I came back here."

"What time?"

"I don't remember." Impatiently. "Does it matter?"

"Yes."

"They were going into dinner already. It must have been after six thirty. The girl on the desk will remember. I asked her to put in a call to England for me."

"She does remember, signora. It is you we are asking."

"Well, that's the best I can do for you. Somewhere after six thirty. But what is all this? Why waste time on what I've been doing, when there is so much I have to tell you."

"Such as—"

"What I didn't manage to tell my—Signor Rivers. That I have been getting anonymous letters. That they brought me here. That I am afraid they are connected with the kidnapping."

"You have them with you?"

"In my room."

"Perhaps we could see them?"

"Of course." Rising to fetch them, she was irritated to find the younger policeman holding the door for her, and then, without a word, coming too. "This is necessary?" She turned on him in the lobby, aware of the girl at the desk, watching avidly.

"Unless you have any strong objection."

"We've wasted enough time as it is." She picked up her key from the desk and led the way upstairs and across the bridge to her room. She went straight to the gimcrack writing table under the window and pulled open the top drawer. "That's funny." She could have sworn she had tucked the packet of letters, in its anonymous linen bag, under her handkerchiefs. But maybe it was under her stockings. She pulled out a side drawer . . . another . . . another. Nothing.

Ridiculous. And ridiculous too to let herself imagine that this was what the young policeman had expected. He stood there, silent, while she went quickly through the drawers of the combined cupboard and wardrobe and then, in a last absurd hope, through her suitcase itself, where it stood behind the door. Then she stood up and faced him. "They've been taken."

"Taken?"

"I had them in that top drawer. I knew it, really. Only, I couldn't believe—"

"You had better come back and tell the boss." Was it her imagination, or did he walk a little closer to her this time?

"They were gone?" The other man did not sound surprised. "There were valuables with them, perhaps?"

"No, I don't travel with valuables."

"Very wise. So—why would anyone take them?"

"Anyone could have." She did not like her own defensive tone. "All the keys in that wing are interchangeable."

"Yes, perhaps. If there *were* any letters?" It was a question.

"Of course there were." She had never shown the letters to Tarn. To prove their existence would mean invoking Sir Charles in England. All the time, precious minutes were ebbing away. "You'll have to take my word for them," she said impatiently. "There are copies in England. In the meantime, what are you doing to find my child?"

"Searching for him," said the older policeman.

"Well, thank God for that."

"But it's not easy in a place like Venice. Very much better to start at the other end, with the kidnappers. You quarreled with Signor Rivers twice yesterday." Again, it was not a question.

"I suppose you could say so. He would not let me see Dominic. I was going to tell him about the letters, to warn him something was going on. But we were interrupted." Suddenly she remembered that feeling she had had as she waited outside Breckon's house, of being watched, spied upon. The Miss Browns, of course, as Tarn had suggested. "By two women." The thoughts had raced through her mind. "I think you should investigate them. Their name is Brown. They said they had a message for my husband from his family."

"Ex-husband," said the policeman.

"Of course." Impatience rose in her throat like bile. "If you would only *listen*. The Miss Browns are leaving today, or so they said. If you waste no time. . . . My ex-husband would probably know where they are staying."

"But Signor Rivers has disappeared," said the older policeman.

"What?"

"You are the last person to have seen him."

"And quarreled with him," added the other.

"Dear God! But how?"

"If we knew that, we would be getting somewhere. All that the girl, Lucia Capella, knew was that he was coming here, to see you, and that he was furiously angry. That is correct?"

"Yes. He thought I had been behind the child's disappearance. I think he was just beginning to believe me when I was called to the phone."

"To believe you?"

"That I had nothing to do with it, of course. I'd just begun to tell him about the letters—"

"The letters that have vanished."

"Yes. Don't you see? It all hangs together. He had a note while I was telephoning. It must have given him a clue—an assignation, even." She was shivering convulsively as the full terror of it hit her. First Dominic, now Breckon.

"A note?" said the older policeman.

"Yes. I told you. He had it in his hand as he crossed the lobby. While I was on the telephone. Lots of people must have seen him. The place was crowded."

"No one remembers."

"The girl at the desk should. The messenger must have asked her—" She paused. "That's funny."

"Precisely. Your ex-husband was not a guest here. How would anyone have found him?"

"They must have followed him. Waited, perhaps, until I was called away."

"Unless you gave him the note, signora."

"I?" As the full horror of it hit her she sank into the chair the younger policeman pushed forward. If they wasted their time on her, what hope for Breckon and Dominic? "You must believe me! I had nothing to do with it." Quickly, desperately, she told them about Sir Charles and her attempt to telephone him the night before. Did they believe her? At least, at last, they left, promising they would telephone Sir Charles for confirmation of her story.

"And you will not leave Venice." It was an order.

"Of course not. It's my *child!*"

"And your ex-husband."

Nine

LEFT ALONE in the dreary little room, Julia bit her nails, a habit of which she had been ruthlessly cured ten years before. Breckon and Dominic. Dominic and Breckon. All my pretty ones. Unlucky to quote *Macbeth*. "Yes?" She turned as the girl from the desk looked in and, automatically, switched off the light.

"There was a telephone call for you, signora, while the police were here. I told the signor you were busy."

"Thank you." Tarn, of course.

"He gave me a message." She had written it down

carefully in her flowing Italian hand. "Sorry to miss you. Author trouble. Campo Morosini. Six o'clock. Don't forget."

The opera. *Turandot.* She had forgotten. And presumably Tarn was out for the day with his Mr. Heyward. So no help from him. She would have to meet him at six, to tell him what happened. Would she be followed by a policeman? She wondered, wryly. And, on the thought, decided that her next move must be a cable to Sir Charles. And not from the hotel desk, either. She had seen the general post office somewhere between Campo Morosini and St. Mark's and now found it easily enough. Drafting the cable was more difficult, but this was no time to economise. She sent Sir Charles the kind of report she would have made, as his assistant, then emerged into brilliant sunshine and an empty day.

Absurd. She would begin by visiting Lucia Capella. But Breckon's house seemed, if possible, more closed and silent than yesterday. She rang twice, and was turning despondently away when the younger policeman appeared, apparently from nowhere. "No use, signora." His tone was almost friendly. "The maid has left and Signorina Capella has gone home to her family."

"Oh. Where?"

"In Venice Mestre. I regret, I do not know the address."

True or false, it was at least courteous, and she thanked him from her heart. "You really are searching?"

"Naturally. But it is not easy, here in Venice."

"And you're wasting your time on me."

He shrugged, neither confirming nor denying it. "Well." She looked at her watch impatiently. It was three o'clock, and she actually was hungry. "I am now about to eat something. Then I shall go back to the Da Rimini in the hope of a message. I shall stay there until a quarter to six, when I shall go to a café in the Campo Morosini, where I am to meet a friend. He is supposed to be taking me to the opera tonight, but I shall not go."

"A friend? One may ask who?"

"I suppose you can ask anything. I met him on the train." Angrily, she felt herself colouring. "I told him about Dominic. He has been helping me. His name is Tarn Menzies."

"He has seen the letters, perhaps?" The hopeful tone made her suddenly and happily suspect that the young policeman was almost on her side, or would like to be.

"No," she said regretfully. And then, suddenly remembering, "But I showed him my little boy's picture. He spotted the house, too."

"A picture?"

Incredible to have forgotten that the picture, at least, was safe in her bag. She reached in and produced it. "They sent me this," she said. "In one of the letters."

"Yes." He studied it. "It's the child. We have, of course, other pictures. But"—regretfully—"you cannot prove that you did not take it yourself. One did not need to be in the garden."

"Signor Menzies will tell you."

"What you told him."

"Yes." It was not evidence, and she knew it. "But you'll talk to him?"

"Naturally. The name of his hotel?"

"He's out for the day." If only Tarn had told her

where he was taking his author.

"You trust him?" The young policeman had anticipated her thinking by a hairsbreadth.

Tarn on the train. The Miss Browns on the train. That scene with the girl. Could it have been faked? She remembered her last glimpse of Pamela spread-eagled on the platform, and shivered. If it had been faked, these were people who took appalling chances. The young policeman was watching her, apparently trying to follow her thoughts. "I . . . don't know," she said slowly. "I thought I did. Could you have someone check up on him?"

"Well." Suddenly, surprisingly, he looked guilty. "There is a difficulty. You see, I was not supposed to speak to you."

"Oh." Here was a difficulty indeed. He had spoken to her because he was sorry for her. She must be grateful, and she must not get him into trouble. "I do see." She looked at her watch again. "Then it will have to wait until you see me meet him this evening, won't it?"

"Yes." In his turn he was grateful. "It's not long. And you do not seriously suspect this Signor Menzies of being involved? It seems to me," he went on gallantly, "that it is more likely to be an involvement of the heart."

"Why, thank you." Once again she felt the little, unwonted surge of confidence Tarn had given her, the young soldiers in the train, and now this very young policeman. "I'm glad you're following me," she said, turned, and left him.

Over a belated sandwich and coffee she searched her heart about her relationship with Tarn and came to no conclusion. Had she taken him, absurdly, on trust, or was she now being just as absurdly suspicious? It is very difficult to be certain on such a point when one's own self-confidence is at so low an ebb as hers had been when she first met Tarn. And, how odd, she thought, despite everything. I *am* better. He's done that for me. So—surely, he must be genuine?

True, false. False, true. And all the time the nagging anxiety for Breckon and Dominic occupied her imagination, clouded her thought. It was four o'clock. She finished her coffee, paid her bill, and hurried back to the Da Rimini, without a backward glance for the young policeman who must be following. And how awkward, she thought, such a pursuit must be in Venice's narrow alleys, with their sudden side-turnings and secret doorways. It was really rather reassuring to think of that friendly young man following, and she slowed her steps slightly, for fear, she was afraid, of losing him.

For once, the girl at the hotel desk had two messages for her; one, at least, an international cable. But its contents were bitterly disappointing. SIR CHARLES AWAY, it ran unhelpfully, WILL GIVE HIM YOUR MESSAGE WHEN HE RETURNS. Signed by his secretary, of course. I made a mistake about that secretary, she told herself, unfolding the second message. It was from Tarn: *"Sorry to miss you. Change of plan. More author trouble!!! Meet me at seven, where we ate last time?"* She had not seen his handwriting before, but it was like him, bold, black, and abrupt. Like him, and unlike those fussy little line drawings of his. He had never shown her a finished one, but the beginnings were curiously amateurish. Like his efforts to recapture that lost

Australian accent? Or—invent it? What had her mind been doing? Suddenly, the facts she had detailed in her cable to Sir Charles shook themselves and fell into shape, the shape in which he would see them. Assume that Tarn was the enemy, the ruthless enemy. What then? She was in her room now, sitting on the bed, staring at the wall, clearing her mind of everything, even of her grinding anxiety for Dominic and Breckon.

First, she made herself look again at that scene back at Victoria. Imagine that it *had* been rigged, that the girl, Pamela, had been bribed to play her part. But—to risk her life and end up in the hospital? She shut her eyes to resee the episode. Why had she not thought to do this before? Well, now? Tarn had tried to hold the girl back. Had held her back? Had held her back until the last possible moment, then pushed? It would account for everything. Reseeing the girl on the platform, now, she saw surprise as well as shock on the blanched face. So, Tarn a double-crosser. It made horrible sense.

Then, go on. If he had known the train was fully booked, and had arranged her own lack of reservation, how easy to have bribed the couchette and wagon-lits attendants and thus ensure their "accidental" meeting. And, she, Sir Charles' girl, had fallen for the lot of it. She had let him lead her by the nose, with his fake Australian and phoney flattery. She was hot and cold at once, with a mixture of shame, anger, and pure terror, as she thought of it. The trouble was, fatally, she had needed the flattery. Had he known that too? He had known altogether too much about her, this anonymous enemy of hers. Tarn Menzies! And she had bought that too, with its hint of a connection with the ex-Prime Minister of Australia.

The Miss Browns had to be in it. It must have been them she had felt watching her as she rang Breckon's doorbell. They had appeared so pat on their cue to prevent any possible understanding or *éclaircissement* between her and Breckon. And Tarn, in his turn, had arrived at the Da Rimini to sweep her off to Torcello before she could make another attempt at warning Breckon about the letters.

If only she had followed through from her doubts about Tarn's fake Australian last night. And why had she not? Because of the attack, of course, and his gallant defense of her. Gallant? Organised, no doubt, when he went to make that telephone call to "author Heyward." He had been furious after the attack. Not, as she had thought, because of it, but because his hired muggers had hit him too hard and made his nose bleed. She shivered a little, counting up the numbers of the enemy. Four of them last night, because, of course, the "chance" water taxi had to be part of the plan. And the Miss Browns. And Peter and Sue, who had provided that timely lift back from Torcello? And, almost certainly, the staff here at the hotel, or some of them. No wonder her call to Sir Charles had not got through. Idiotic not to have thought of that sooner. If I get out of this, she thought, I will retire and grow cabbages.

But would she get out? And, far more important, would Breckon and Dominic? Whatever Tarn's plans for them, he meant her to look responsible. The police were half convinced of it already. Would they believe her if she went to them and accused Tarn? It seemed highly unlikely. And Sir Charles was away. No use trying to telephone him, even if she dared do so from that exposed, hostile hotel desk. She sat down at her rickety dressing table and made a brief abstract in Italian of her suspicions. Her friendly policeman would be waiting to follow her out to dinner with Tarn. She would manage to give it to him first, then if anything happened to her this evening. . . .

But why should it? She was to be the scapegoat. And it was time to dress. In a spirit of defiance she put on the one brightly coloured garment she had brought, a long patchwork skirt that made her at least look as if she meant to go to the opera. Because—she was buttoning the black shirt that went with the skirt—at all costs she must not let Tarn see that she suspected him. If she could only reverse their roles, he might, somehow, give her a clue to where Dominic and Breckon were.

Time to go. Locking her room door behind her, she remembered the stolen letters and grimaced at the waste of time. It was darker than usual in the corridor, and when she emerged on to the bridge that joined the annex to the hotel itself, she saw why. The light that hung from its vine-covered trellis was out. She must tell the girl at the desk. It was not absolutely dark yet, but she would not like to come this way when it was. As she closed the annex door behind her, the warning shrieked in her mind. Had she let Tarn out-think her once again? She would take no chances, but buzz the desk from her room. Her hand was back on the door, feeling for the handle to reopen it, when something came down, smothering, over her head, and, cursing herself, she fell into blackness.

She was lying, face down, awkwardly cramped. Above her an engine hummed. A boat, moving fast. Not a *vaporetto*. Something small. A water taxi? She was so numb from the drug she must have been given, and from her cramped position in the bottom of the boat, that it took her a few minutes to realise her hands were tied behind her back. She wriggled a little, trying to turn over, and a voice spoke above her. "Blast!"

Tarn. It was all true, every black, incredible suspicion. She made herself lie still and pretended unconsciousness while she faced it, cleared her mind, and thought back to unshuffle the whole pack of disaster. She had been right, but right too late. Tarn was indeed the enemy. Ahead of her as always, he had snatched her from the bridge over that dark cul-de-sac at the Da Rimini. Worst of all, the friendly young policeman would doubtless still be waiting, cold and impatient and full of suspicion, at the front of the hotel. How long would he wait? What would he do? Even if he went on believing in her, which seemed unlikely, he would be hamstrung by the fact that he could not admit he had spoken to her. No hope there. In fact, danger. What had happened to her bag with the document she had drafted so carefully for the police? Thank God, she remembered dropping it in the shock of the attack. No reason, surely, why Tarn should have bothered to pick it up.

So no reason why she should not go on playing the idiot. There might even be a marginal advantage in doing so. It should be easy enough, God knew. "Tarn?" She made the question hopeful, and then, wriggling in the bottom of the boat, which she now recognised as a very expensive private one: "Thank God, is it really you?"

"I wouldn't start cheering yet." Tarn had dropped the Australian accent and now spoke with just a trace of a South Carolina drawl. And there was something else in his voice. Triumph. Vicious, unmistakable triumph. "Easy, weren't you, girl?" On the word, he switched back to the Australian accent. "Word of a 'Strine, I thought I'd kill myself trying not to laugh. Sir Charles' prize pupil falling for the oldest trick in the world. Perfect little setup, weren't you?" She felt his hands at work above her, and the boat moved faster, but still quietly on expensively silenced engines. "Don't waste your breath screaming, girl. No one will hear. There's no one *to* hear."

"But, Tarn, I don't understand." If he went on thinking her the fool she had been, he might say something, do something. . . . It was the forlornest of hopes, and she knew it.

"Not Tarn." Mocking laughter, rippling through the voice above her, sent a cold prickle of absolute terror down her spine. "Let me introduce myself, Cousin. Antony Rivers."

"Rivers?" Her mind scrabbled frantically for explanations.

"A tainted Rivers." He was licking his chops on it. "One of the doomed ones, Cousin Julia. Only we—my father and I—we have always intended to enjoy our doom."

"Your father?"

"Uncle Paul to you. One does have a father, you know." He laughed, not pleasantly. "Tough, aren't you? I thought we'd given you enough to keep you unconscious, but now you're here, it's kind of fun to tell you. We can easily put you out again, when the time comes."

"We?"

"Purely a manner of speaking. The royal Rivers we, if you like. The others have something else to do. Oh, my oath, they have. Do you know," he went on, enjoying himself, "it's the first time I've ever used the name. I think I like it. I think I'm glad you woke up, Cousin Julia."

"Don't call me that."

"Why not? It's true enough. And legitimate." He brought it out with a kind of bravado. "God, I was angry at first. All that time in the orphanage . . . treated as a bastard . . . 'parentage unknown.' Christ, when Paul told me, I nearly killed him. But he was right, of course. He'd thought of everything. Even down to drama lessons." He lapsed for a moment, horribly, into the Australian accent, then modulated back to the Southern drawl. "Of course, I'd not have had to use it if it hadn't been for you." Venom in his voice now. "When Paul first told me who I was, he thought he had it all sewed up. The lot of them convinced they must never marry. Well, easy enough with the other three. All Raoul wanted was his bottle and who'd have had Mandy or Fan? Breckon took more convincing, but Paul thought he had it made. I bet he never told you about his fits."

"Breckon?"

"Thought he hadn't. Easy enough to induce, with the right drugs. Mother provided them, natch."

"Your mother?"

"Matron Andrews, of course. I'm not sure it wasn't

all her idea in the first place. There's a woman for you. Sat quiet all those years, acting the starched spinster, waiting. Then, when the time came, she was going to come forward, marriage lines in one hand, my birth certificate in the other. Never had the nerve to tell Paul about me, because of the taint. See? Stayed near because she loved him. Natch? Loved me too, couldn't raise me; did her best. Convincing, too. That woman loves nothing and nobody but Madam Andrews." He spoke it with full and deep admiration, then laughed. "Well, look at the way she put the Indian sign on that poor old fool McCartland. God, she was furious when she found he'd crossed her up and not sterilised you when she told him to. Old fool. 'Sanctity of human life. . . . Tampering with nature.' Pity, he was useful, but I'll deal with him when I get back. That should be kind of fun, too."

He's mad, she thought. He's cold, clean mad. And, horribly: it's true about the taint. "Where are you taking me?" It was all too easy to sound the cowed victim.

"Shall I tell you?" The engine note fell as he slowed down. "I don't see why not." He enjoyed the idea. "You'll have fun explaining to darling Breckon when he comes to. *If* he does."

"What have you done to him?"

"He hit his head when he fell into the barge, poor Cousin Breckon. It made it all very easy. Not a squeak out of him. Our Miss Brown packs quite a punch. Regular spitfire the police are going to think you. Off your rocker, of course. Caught it from Breckon? Mad about the child? I don't care what they think so long as no one thinks of me. And why should they? I don't exist." The engine slowed down a little more. "Pity I can't mark you, but can't be sure how the accident is going to work. I've owed you something for yesterday."

"Yesterday? Accident?"

"Getting that lift back from Torcello." He sounded furious at the memory. "Balling up my plans. God, we improvised neatly, though. And fast! Breckon was to have been taken while you were on your way to meet me tonight," he explained. "And you on your way back from the opera. . . . No time for the police to get on to you. But this way's better. They've talked to you, haven't they? Didn't believe you, did they? Not when you couldn't produce my letters. God, what a lovely little fool you were. Walked right into the hotel we booked you and never thought about the staff. I've enjoyed playing with you, Cousin Julia."

"What are you going to do now?" This was the moment, she knew, even through her own rage with herself, to ask the question.

"Not much. Put you out again. Dump you on my island. You can nurse Breckon for me. He needs to be alive when you kill him."

"I?"

"Well, natch. What do you think I've gone to all this trouble for? You're going to kill them both. Cousin Breckon and darling little cripple Dominic. Oh, a terrible accident, it's going to be. Maybe I won't tell you just how it's going to work, but you've got enough of a brain to see the logic of it. You kidnapped Dominic. Right? Breckon got on to it. Right? He followed you, caught up, there was a row. Disaster. Bang go the bunch of you. Work it out for yourself.

A boat, maybe? A fight? No prizes for the right answer."

Through the fear, the rage, the fury with herself, she was aware of something else. A light ahead. Perhaps a string of lights? The posts that marked the channel to Torcello? Very quietly, very carefully, she gathered herself together. Not a hope of getting overboard, but if she should just stand up, show herself, scream?

"You're not all that stupid." His voice, from above her, was almost regretful. "I've enjoyed our little talk. But, now, good-bye, girl." His pounce was so swift the needle was in her arm before she could even try to evade it.

"Are you all right? Can you hear me?" Something cold on her forehead. The child's voice, anxious, above her. With an immense effort, she opened her eyes. He was hanging over her, Dominic, her son. "Oh, good. You're better." While she searched for words, he put the cold, wet cloth gently back on her forehead. "Do you think you can move? It's cold for you on the grass. I couldn't move you. I tried. I've only got one good hand, you see, and I'm not very big."

"Dominic!" For courage like his, one could do anything. She rolled sideways and sat up, her hands still, awkwardly, tied behind her.

"You know my name?" The next question followed with appalling logic. "Who are you?"

"Your mother, Dominic. I'm not dead. I—lost you." No time for this, and no need. They had recognised each other. "Where's your father?"

"In the shed." Like her, he seemed to feel there was no time for anything but facts. "The man put him there.

He said he wanted him alive. Mother——" It was, extraordinarily, both acknowledgment and appeal. "What's happening?"

"Nothing good, I'm afraid. Except seeing you." She leaned up towards him, the effort making her head swim, and, understanding, he bent his small height down to meet her kiss. "Dominic." She said it again, with love. "Help me up, my darling, and let's see how your father is."

"Your hands first," he said. "I've got my penknife. It's a good one. Father always gives good things. They didn't search me." He needed to talk about it. "One of them said, 'Shall I go over him?' and the other, the boss, kind of laughed, and said, 'No need, a cripple like him.' "

"Oh, Dominic." Tears filled her eyes.

"Don't cry," said the extraordinarily adult child's voice. "I don't think we have time." He put his good left hand into an inner pocket of his scarlet windbreaker and produced a magpie collection of small objects. Matches, hairpins, a paperclip, a long piece of string, and, at last, a serviceable pocket knife. "Hold still. It may take me a little while."

"You can't untie them?" She was furious with herself as she said it.

"I'm afraid not." It was courteous, regretful, matter-of-fact. "My hand doesn't look too bad now, but it's not much use." He opened the knife with his teeth and held it carefully between the good and bad hand. "I'll try not to cut you."

They were both silent while he sawed patiently away at the tough cord, and it gave her time to realise how long she must have been unconscious. It was morning light that showed her ragged grass and desolate buildings, and, curtailing everything, a strongly built wall. The knife slipped and cut her.

"Oh, Mother!"

"It's nothing. Keep going, Dominic. My fault, I must have moved."

"You didn't." His voice told of a million compromises refused. This child of hers—of Breckon's—was the most amazing person she had ever met. More than she deserved? What had she to do with it?

"There," he said triumphantly as the last strand parted. "Let me rub them for you. He'd tied them horribly tight. It's not much of a cut, is it?"

"Nothing," she reassured him. The watch on her wrist had stopped. "What time is it, Dominic?"

"Early. Ten past seven. He must have brought you when it was still dark. He doesn't come in the daytime. I think we must be quite near the *vaporetto* channel. I wish I'd found you sooner. Are you very cold?"

"I've been warmer." She also had a throbbing headache, the aftermath, presumably, of whatever drug Tarn had given her, but no need to tell Dominic that. "So he won't come again till dark?"

"That's it. He brought me the night before last. I tried to keep track of where we were going, but it was hard, down in the bottom of the boat. Only, I do know we crossed the main *vaporetto* channel quite soon before we landed here. They'd given me something that put me to sleep, only I waked up in the boat. I didn't let on, though."

"Sensible. There." She had been rubbing her ice-cold feet with stiff hands. "I think I can move now. Take me to your father, Dominic. When did they bring him?"

"Much later the same night. I hoped at first they'd come take me away, but they just dumped him on the cot and went. There's no light," he explained. "But they had flashlights. I tried to wake Father after they went, but he just groaned. And—I didn't want to use all my matches. He's breathing, though." He anticipated her terror. "This way." He took her right hand with his left one to lead her through tangled grass and weeds towards a building that leaned up against one of the island's claustrophobic surrounding walls. "I'm afraid you'll get your skirt wet."

"It's wet already." But she hitched it up with her other hand. What an extraordinary child he was, with his adult speech, his grave courtesy, and his apparently total acceptance of the fact of her. This told her something heartwarming, too, about Breckon. Dominic had clearly heard nothing against her. She had, simply, been dead.

The shed had once been a house of some kind. It had a door, and windows of sorts, and morning sunshine, just beginning to take some of the damp chill from the air, showed rudimentary furnishings. Breckon was lying on an army cot, not, as she had feared, on the cold ground. "They said they wanted him alive." Dominic had an uncanny trick of reading one's thoughts. "There's food, too, and water. For another day."

"I see." She knew that he did, too. Something was going to happen to them tonight. She bent over Breckon, wishing she had paid more attention to the first-aid course Sir Charles had made her take. He had hit his head, Tarn had told her. So—concussion. What in the world did one do for that? But Dominic had been right in his reassurance. Breckon was breathing easily enough, and his forehead was almost too cool to her touch. The bump on the side of his head was large, but not, she thought, alarmingly so. "He's cold," she said.

"There's only one blanket. I doubled it, but it's not much."

She looked about the dreary little room, wondering where he had slept, and saw her answer in a pile of straw in one corner. She thought about rats, wondered if he had, and could not control a long, slow shudder. Well, they would be lucky if they were here tonight. "You're sure there's no way we can get off the island?"

"I don't think there is." Dominic's eyes were huge with anxiety. "I went all round the wall yesterday. Only, of course, I had to keep coming back to see if Father—"

"Yes. Well, today we can take it in turns." But they both knew they would not have been on this island if escape from it had been possible.

"There's a water gate." Once again, Dominic answered her question before she had asked it. "They bring the boat right in. I heard them when they brought Father. I was in bed." His eyes slid from the cot where Breckon lay to a half-open cupboard door. "I got out and hid. They didn't bother to look for me. Just said 'We'll find him quick enough when we need him,' dumped Father on the cot and left. I'd seen it was Father, so at least I wasn't afraid anymore. Except about him."

She swallowed tears. The admission of fear was almost braver than she could bear. "What is there for breakfast, Dominic?" she asked. "I'm famished."

"Good." His smile, the first one, turned her heart upside down. "You'll need to be. Rolls, and more rolls, cheese and fruit. And water."

"Delicious. Let's take it outside, shall we? I think it's warmer out than in already. I wish we could get your father out."

"When he comes to, we will. He looks much better this morning."

"Does he?" Extraordinary to be drawing her strength from him. More extraordinary still to realise, as they began to carry out their frugal picnic into the sun, how little, already, she noticed the fact of his bad hand. By an adept use of the good one to pass things to the other, he seemed to be carrying almost more than his fair share of the load.

Settled in the sunshine, on a bit of decayed terrace, he looked up at her with a sudden challenge in his smile. "Shall I peel you an apple?" asked her son.

Ten

THE EXQUISITELY peeled apple set the tone for that whole extraordinary day. After finishing their picnic breakfast, they made the tour of the island together, having agreed, solemnly, that Breckon was sleeping quietly enough to be left alone. The walls were continuous, solid, and impossibly high. The water gate, when they reached it on the far side of the island, was equally solid, and inaccessible from the land, since it guarded a deep, walled channel that ran up to a disused landing place. "I've looked at it as well as I could," Dominic said. "And you can see it's got a huge bolt on the other side. No use to swim out to it. I swim very well," he told her.

"Do you, Dominic? It's more than I do." What did he *not* do well, this child she had given away?

"I wish I could play the piano." He might have been reading her thoughts. And then, "Funny, I never told Father that."

For the second time, she fought back tears. Then, "There are piano arrangements for one hand, I think. Duets, mostly. I play a little. We could . . ." She bit off the end of the sentence.

"We need to get out of here," said Dominic. "I'll tell you one thing, Mother. There's a tree on that little hill in the middle of the island. It doesn't show much because it's in among the bushes. I tried to climb it yesterday, but it's difficult with one hand. If you could give me a leg up? I think, from the top, I might be able to see over the wall."

"Let's go."

"You'll tear your pretty skirt."

She looked down at the bright patchwork that had dried already in the morning sun. "That's just what I'm going to do. Lend me your penknife, Dominic?"

They made a rough enough job of it, but it was a blessed relief to find herself free-moving in a jagged-edged, knee-length skirt. "And I expect the pieces will come in handy for something," said Dominic.

He had found a comparatively easy way through the thick growth of bushes, and Julia kept close behind him, grateful for her flat-heeled evening sandals. The hill, masked by the bushes, was higher than she had realised, and when they stopped under a scrubby-looking oak tree she saw that Dominic was very likely right. From its top—if one could only get there—it might well be possible to see over the wall.

They stood and looked at it for a moment. Growing up from among the undergrowth, it had put out no sideways branches until it reached daylight, a little above Julia's head. "I'm very light," said Dominic.

"And I'm quite strong. But you'll be careful, won't you?"

"I'm always careful. You have to be, with only one good hand. If I know I can't, I won't try."

"Dominic!"

"Yes?" He looked up at her with those huge brown eyes, so like Breckon's.

"No." She smiled down at him. "Not now. Later . . . perhaps."

"Perhaps," he agreed gravely, and let her pick him up. He was light, agonisingly so, and she had a sudden, sharp memory of the only other time she had held him, when they had brought him to her in the hospital to prove that she must let him go. Now, she dared not hold him for more than a moment, for fear of incapacitating tears. But if he could be brave, so, God help her, could she.

"Fine." The tree trunk was small enough so that he could get his left arm around it. He began a curious, scrambling ascent into its thick upper growth, while Julia stood below, following his progress anxiously, praying that she would be able to catch him, or at least break his fall, if he should lose his grip.

Soon he was out of sight among thickly growing leaves, but his voice came down to her reassuringly.

"It gets easier up here." And then, excited. "Yes! I can see." The tree rustled violently.

"Do be careful!" She could not help it.

And, "I am careful," he told her again. The rustling stopped, but she could see that the whole tree was swaying. He must be very high up indeed. Suppose it gave way. On the thought, she heard him begin to come back down, and breathed a sigh of relief.

"Wow!" He sounded, for once, like a little boy, as his flushed face appeared among the branches above her. "That was fun. Like being at the masthead in a gale maybe? I didn't think I'd better stay more than a minute—pity to wreck the tree. I had to go quite high."

"I thought you did." She reached up to catch him as he turned and let himself down by his good arm from the lowest branch. Putting the featherweight down, she saw that his face was covered with scratches, some of them bleeding. "Oh, Dominic!" Miraculously, she still had her handkerchief, and dabbed very gently at the worst of them.

"It's nothing." He sounded impatient for the first time, and she realised that he had no proper spare hand to protect himself.

"No, they're not bad," she agreed, "but let's go back and wash them just the same."

"And see how Father is."

"Yes." They were moving already, back along the path they had trodden through the bushes. "But, now, what did you see?"

"First of all, we're not a bit far from the main channel to Torcello. Remember, I thought so? And we must be on the land side. I saw a plane going down to the airport. And that's not all. There's another island, quite near—with a boat."

"And a house?"

"I couldn't see. If there is, it must be on the other side. There are cypresses. I think there must be a house."

"Theirs?" She knew he shared her fear. "How far is it, Dominic? I mean, if it wasn't theirs, could we signal, or shout, or something?"

"I don't see how."

Nor did she. Besides, it seemed so horribly likely that Tarn and his accomplices were using the other island as their headquarters. "If there's a boat, there has to be someone on the island," she said.

"No." He smiled his brilliant upward smile. "They might have two boats."

"Of course. Stupid of me." They had reached the shed and, entering first, she forgot everything else at the sight of Breckon sitting shakily upright on the cot, his legs over the side.

"You!" He struggled to his feet at sight of her. "If you've hurt him, I'll—I'll—"

"Don't, Father." Dominic, who had come quietly in behind her, spoke protectively. "It's Mother, don't you see?"

"I certainly do. But how do you—"

"I told him, of course." There was no time for this. Julia moved forward to put a hand on Breckon's forehead. "You're better?"

"Yes." He looked at the two of them, standing there, side by side. "I don't understand anything. You mean"—his face changed—"you mean it wasn't you, Julia?"

"Of course not," said Julia, and, simultaneously, "She was dumped here in the night," said Dominic. "I found her this morning."

"They drugged me," said Julia. "Breckon, I've been every kind of fool you like, from start to finish, but you've got to believe that I've had nothing to do with any of this. Except by *being* a fool and letting it happen."

He sat down again, shakily, on the cot. "I wish I understood. Can't even remember what happened to me."

"Come out into the sun," said Dominic. "Are you hungry? You ought to be. I'll peel you an apple." Dropping Julia's hand, he took Breckon's and pulled him gently out into the now hot sun. "That's better, isn't it? Here—" He picked up the rest of Julia's skirt from where they had left it. "Sit on this. The grass is still damp."

"Your skirt?" Breckon was looking at Julia now as if he really saw her for the first time. "I never thought I'd see you in rags."

"I never thought I'd see you again."

"And here we are." Dominic had fetched an apple from the shed and was deftly peeling it, as he had Julia's. Now he passed a piece to his father, who ate it obediently, while Julia thought how strangely the father-child relationship seemed to have reversed itself. "Where are we?" A little colour was creeping back into Breckon's face.

"On an island in the lagoon," Julia told him. "It's walled all round. I can't think why, but it means we can't get off."

"It will be one of the ones they used for ammunition

dumps." Breckon ate another piece of apple, silently handed to him by Dominic. "In the war. But—why?"

"It's a long story," said Julia. How could she tell it in front of Dominic?

He read her mind once again. "I've got an idea." He stood up. "Back in a minute."

"You'll be careful," said Breckon, and, "I'm always careful," Dominic told him, as he had Julia.

Let alone, they looked at each other, for a long moment, quite silent. Then, "He's wonderful," said Julia. "I . . . I . . . I do thank you, Breckon," and then, quickly, before he could interrupt her. "Oh, I know you didn't do it for me, but I thank you just the same. He's—extraordinary."

"I think so." Absentmindedly he reached out, picked up a roll Dominic had left beside him on the grass, and began to eat it, hungrily. "How you could—"

"I had a breakdown." They were talking in a kind of shorthand, well aware they had no time to waste. "Breckon, you've got to listen—and believe me. For Dominic's sake. I've wanted to die often enough. I don't mind so much. Not with you two. But—he's too valuable. He wants to play the piano," she said, as if it explained everything.

"He never told me that." He reached out and took her hand, almost as if he was feeling some moral pulse. "He trusts you."

"Yes."

"Then, so do I." The grip on her hand changed, became friendly. "So, tell me your story quickly, Julia, if it's as bad as I think."

"Yes. Mind you, he knows—Dominic—but, just the same. . . ."

"We're to be killed." It was hardly a question.

"Tonight I think. I don't know how, but it's going to look my fault. That I kidnapped Dominic . . . you came after us . . something happened. And that's the lot of us gone—out of the way."

"But, Julia, in the name of God, why?"

"That's where you've got to believe me, though I can hardly believe it myself. You've got a cousin, Breckon. Uncle Paul's son. His legitimate son. I think he's mad."

"Uncle Paul? Married?"

"Yes. To Miss Andrews. You remember? The matron at St. Helen's. Years ago. Secretly. He didn't tell me why."

"Who didn't tell you?"

"Breckon!" She kneeled up to face him. "This is where you have to try and believe me. And forgive me. I can't forgive myself. Never. Well—I shan't have long."

"Tonight, you think?" To this extent, at least, he seemed, mercifully, to be believing her.

"It has to be. I cabled Sir Charles yesterday." It seemed light-years ago. "He was away, but he's never out of touch for long. When he gets it, he'll come. They'll know that. They won't risk waiting. Why should they? I keep hoping for a helicopter. But we can't count on it."

"No," said Breckon. And then, almost casually: "I was always jealous of Sir Charles."

"I know. Now. Uncle Paul put it into your head, didn't he? I realised when Tarn was talking to me."

"Tarn?"

"Your cousin. Paul's son. The enemy."

His hand tightened on hers, hard. "So, what were you doing talking to him?"

"You may well ask. He'd fooled me, do you see, upside down, backwards, sideways. If I live to be a hundred, which seems unlikely, I'll never forgive myself. Do you know"—she saw it now, unspeakably too late—"I never realised, but I was a pushover for him because he reminded me of you."

"A pushover? You—Sir Charles' girl?"

"Don't call me that! He did. Tarn. Don't you see? That's what Uncle Paul did. It has to be. Put it into your head. Made you jealous. So you wouldn't believe me, back at La Rivière. Think, Breckon. Try and remember."

He hated it. She could see that, but she could also see that he was trying. "Yes," he said at last. "It's true. But it was so cleverly done. I loved Uncle Paul." She noticed the past tense, and rejoiced. "Do you remember that time when Sir Charles came to the States and you flew up to New York to help him?"

"Of course I do. His new assistant was ill. It was the least I could do to go and give a hand."

"That's just what Uncle Paul said." Breckon's voice was savage. "It was almost all he said."

"Almost?"

"He said"—Breckon found it hard to get it out—"he said it was a good thing we'd agreed to have no children. And all the time. . . ." His quick mind had been working on it. "He had a son of his own. This Tarn. Who was going to come forward in his own good time, and inherit the whole estate?"

"That's it. Is there so much, Breckon? Is it worth it?"

"Oh, God, yes. Mineral rights. That's why I came away. I couldn't stand what it was doing to them all. And—I wouldn't agree to what they wanted to do. So then, accidents started to happen. To me, this time; and I began to think about you, and yours. To wonder. I came to England to see you, Julia. That's when I learned about Dominic."

"And didn't see me?"

"Not when I heard you were giving him up. They didn't tell me about the breakdown. I wonder why not."

"Did you tell them you were my husband? Had been," she corrected hurriedly.

"No." He saw it. "Of course not. I didn't give a name. I see what you mean. You can't altogether blame them. No business of mine. And very likely Sir Charles had given instructions."

"I'm sure he had." Heartwarming to share his dry tone about Sir Charles and his instructions. "Too capable by a half."

"Yes. So—you were giving away my child. I was damned angry. So angry I managed the adoption in the teeth of all the odds. Well—poor little Dominic— he was a difficult case. Not many would have taken him. And, thank God, I had the money."

"From the mineral rights?"

"No. Don't you understand? I wouldn't let them tear up La Rivière. That's when the 'accidents' started to happen. I'm earning my own now. I'm the most prosperous private accountant in Venice. Or should I say, I was?"

"I hope not. And you shouldn't say, 'poor little Dominic,' either."

"How right you are. He's quite a guy, our son."

"Yes." The warmth of that word "our" glowed in her. "Breckon, you've changed so."

"For the better?" He laughed. "I certainly hope so. Pain in the neck, wasn't I? Everybody's ideal bureaucrat. Stuffed shirt Rivers. I can't think how you stood me."

"I loved you," she said. "I still do. I always will. But—what did it, Breckon? Changed you?"

"Dominic, of course. Did you ever see a stuffed shirt change a diaper and live?"

"You did it yourself?"

"Of course I did. My son, wasn't he? My problem. My fight. Only, somehow, he won. For us both. By being what he is; what you've seen. Extraordinary. Mind you"—there was a smile in his voice—"I didn't always feel like that. There were times. . . . Well, he changed my life. I didn't figure on that when I got him, but of course it happened. You just wait. . . ."

"Wait?"

"Till we have the next one." Now he was laughing. "Will you mind my showing you how to cope with him?"

"Her," she said. And then, "Oh, Breckon. . . ."

"I know. But we're going to make it. Somehow. We have to. We've got so much. And Dominic. Don't cry, darling, here he comes." And then, as she absorbed the extraordinary word. "Dominic! You loon! What have you been doing?"

Dominic, but not his clothes, was wet. His long, golden curls were plastered against his skull, accentuating the likeness to Breckon. But his eyes were shining and his voice triumphant. "Swimming," he said. "I suddenly thought the water gate mightn't go right down, so I went to see, and it doesn't. Someone quite small could dive underneath."

"And then?" asked Breckon.

"I could swim to the next island. Did Mother tell you about it? And get the boat. You know I've driven ours often enough."

"Only out in the lagoon," said Breckon.

"This is out in the lagoon. And besides. . . ." The knowledge of the alternative hung heavily in the air between the three of them.

"How far is it? The other island?" asked Julia.

"Not far. Honest, I could swim it. I've done further at the Lido lots of times. You know, Father."

"He is a strong swimmer," said Breckon, almost reluctantly.

"I'm so little," explained Dominic. "It's easy. And, if I start getting tired, I'll come back. Cross my heart."

"And"—Breckon had thought of something—"if you find you can, when you get under, you'll open the gate?"

"I shan't be able to . . . not from the water. It looks like just a bolt, but it's high up, d'you see?"

Of course, it would be, where it could be reached from a boat. "I don't like it." Julia turned to Breckon. "We thought—Dominic and I—it might be them . . . on the other island. Suppose they hear him?"

"Why should they?" asked Dominic. "I couldn't see the house, if there is one. It has to be the other side of the island."

"And the island is in sight of the main channel to Torcello?" Breckon was summing up the chances in his mind.

"That's right."

"So if they are there, they won't do anything until after dark."

"No," Julia agreed.

"I wish I could see," said Breckon. "Any chance of my climbing your tree, Dominic?"

"It only just held me."

"It's true," said Julia. "I was scared silly."

"Well," Breckon stood up. "Let's take one more look around the walls, just in case there's somewhere. After all, if you do try it, Dominic, dusk's the time." Unspoken between him and Julia was the hope that before then, help might come from Sir Charles, or from the Venetian police, who must, presumably, be looking for all three of them by now. As they started round the walls, Julia told the others about the friendly young policeman who had been assigned to follow her. "The trouble is," she summed up her own fears for them. "He may so easily have thought I'd fooled him—given him the slip to contradict what I'd told him."

"Not encouraging," said Breckon. "And neither is this wall."

"No," Julia agreed. "That's what we thought. And someone's taken a lot of trouble to clear away the bushes alongside of it."

"Someone's taken a lot of trouble," said Breckon.

"There must be a terrible lot of money involved."

"There is. Plenty to pay for a little hired help."

Julia shivered. Bad enough to think of Tarn as the enemy, but behind him stretched a faceless threatening line. No, not entirely faceless. The Miss Browns, she knew, were part of the gang. "The Miss Browns are in it," she said, mainly for something to occupy all their minds.

"Oh! Miss Andrews' nieces. They brought me a message. . . . And—I remember now. I met them. As I was coming away from that hotel of yours, Julia. I'd had a note—it's all coming back." His face changed, as if a shadow had crossed the sun. "While you were on the telephone. A boy brought it. It said: *'She's got him. Don't let her fool you. Come, quick, to the steps of the Spiritu Sanctu. It may not be too late.'* Something like that." He felt in his pockets. "It's gone. But—it enclosed a note from you, Julia."

"From me?"

"Yes. As proof. There was a postscript, saying so. That I ought to know your writing. I do."

"Breckon, you can't believe—" The blazing anger in his face was worse than any blow.

"Hang on," said Dominic. "What did the note say, Father?"

Breckon passed a distracted hand over his forehead. "Let me think. Just a line. *'Take good care of him.'* And that squiggle you always use for a signature to people you know well. What else could I—" He stopped, stared at her with those accusing eyes. "What else can I think?"

"My writing. You're sure?"

"Of course I'm sure. It's no use, Julia. The game's up; whatever it is. You hadn't thought, had you, that it might be dangerous to risk yourself alone with me?"

"And me," said Dominic. And then, as Julia looked at him with horror, thinking that he, too, had turned against her, he asked his question. "What was the paper like, that mother's note was on?"

"Like?" Puzzled. "Oh, yes. . . . There was something odd about it. Yellow, old—as if it had been taken out of an old notebook."

"Or as if it was an old note?" asked Dominic, and, almost at the same moment, "Good God!" said Julia. "Don't you remember, Breckon, that time I had to go to New York, to Sir Charles? You weren't well? You didn't like my going? It was all miserable. I remember writing a note like that, from the airport— to Amanda. Just to make myself feel better. I suppose Uncle Paul must have got hold of it. Dear God. . . ." She looked back with horror down the years of patient treachery.

"You did? That's funny."

"Why?" She hoped he was beginning to believe her, and could see that Dominic thought so too.

"Because I remember Paul saying how odd it was we hadn't heard from you. He made a big thing about it, in a quiet way. I suppose that was when I started. . . ." He was silent, gazing at her with a kind of horror.

"Wondering about me." She finished it for him. "And I don't blame you! I wrote you every day, Breckon. The note to Amanda was enclosed in one to you. From the airport." She coloured, but went bravely on. "There wasn't much time. I just said I loved you."

"It would have been enough. Julia, believe me—I never had any of them."

"I do believe you." She was remembering, coldly, that the mail at La Rivière was all delivered, by prescriptive right, to Uncle Paul, who shared it out among the family. And why not? A loving family. His. "Why didn't you say something when I got back?" she asked now.

"I didn't like to. It . . . would have seemed like

grumbling. Paul said—" He stopped. "God, what a fool I was. Do you remember, that day you were attacked. By the Cooper?"

"I should say!"

"Julia! You'll have to forgive me!" He looked quickly from her to Dominic. "Did you never wonder why I was there? Not at Charleston?"

"Of course I did."

"Well—" He plunged into it, "Uncle Paul said you were meeting someone. By the Cooper. On those morning walks of yours. He—half suggested it was something to do with Sir Charles. Oh—I was crazy even to think of believing him. But—I had to be sure. You oughtn't to forgive me—not really."

"I do," she said. "We were their puppets, weren't we?"

"Yes. Well—I loved Uncle Paul. If it's any excuse. When that tramp was found dead, he said—Uncle Paul—that he must have been the man. The one you'd been meeting. Least said, soonest mended, he said. For your sake. Do you see?"

"Dear God, yes. Clever! I wonder who he was, poor man."

"I've been thinking about that," said Breckon. "Some unlucky wretch from St. Helen's, don't you think? Laid on by Miss Andrews. If I'd only insisted on a proper investigation at the time. . . . But do you see?"

"Uncle Paul made you think it would involve me?"

"Yes. He was so . . . so kind about it. And I let him fool me."

"They're quite a pair, Uncle Paul and his son Tarn." For a moment, Julia forgot the threatening present in her relief at the past explained. "Uncle Paul fooled you. Tarn fooled me. I think we'll just have to forgive each other, darling, don't you? But, tell me. Later, after I'd moved into the hotel. Did you get my letters then?"

"I never had another letter from you, Julia. Only the ones from the lawyers about the divorce."

"They terrify me," said Julia. "All those years. . . . All that wickedness."

"And all our unhappiness," he said. "All that wasted time."

"Do kiss each other if you like," said Dominic. "I don't mind," and was surprised and pleased to find himself simultaneously hugged by both parents, the shared gesture more satisfactory than any kiss.

But Breckon had been thinking about Julia's story.

"Tarn told you all this?" he asked now. "About Uncle Paul and Miss Andrews?"

"Yes." They both knew it for their death sentence. "I think we'll have to let Dominic try and swim for it," she went on. "Don't you?"

"Unless we can think of something else. And if he's going in swimming at teatime, he'd better have some lunch now. Besides, I'm starving."

"You look much better," said Julia.

"I feel it. You're sure I couldn't get under that water gate, Dominic?"

"Quite sure." It was curious, Julia thought, to be so certain this was the truth.

"Dominic," she said. "If you get to the island and can't make the boat start, you'll hide there, won't you? Not swim back?"

"I'll scout around. I might find help." It was not quite an answer, and they all knew it.

Lunch was breakfast all over again, except that the rolls were dryer and the water warm and brackish. And—it finished the supplies.

"I wonder if there's a well on the island," said Breckon.

"You mean—they might just leave us here?"

"Well—it would look a kind of accident, wouldn't it? If the water gate had jammed."

"No boat," said Dominic.

"And what about Sir Charles? Didn't you say he'd come galloping to the rescue, Julia? How much does my cousin Tarn know about him, by the way?"

"Too much by a half." But Julia's heart had leapt at the casual reference to Sir Charles. "The only good thing is he doesn't know I cabled him—and that's only because I never had the chance to tell him—" Fury at her own gullibility curled her voice, "Anyway, I think he might easily have worked out that I would. Just the same, let's see if we can find a well." They all knew that it would be better to be doing something than just sitting and waiting for dusk.

There was no well. They had none of them expected to find one. Julia looked at her watch. "I think Dominic should rest up for that swim."

They lay in the sun, Dominic in the middle, not talking, not sleeping, very content to be together. Only, whenever they heard the sound of a plane to the north where the airport was, a kind of shiver of hope ran through all three of them.

At last a finger of shadow fell across Julia's hand. "Do you think—"

"Yes," said Breckon. "It gets dark so fast. You're sure, Dominic?"

"Quite sure. I'll be careful, I promise I will. Think what a lot I have to be careful for."

"Come on, then." Breckon swung him up on to his shoulders for the walk across the island, and Julia felt a swift, shameful pang of jealousy.

But when they got to the inlet that ran down to the water gate, Dominic turned to her for help with the zip of his red windbreaker. "You won't be too cold?" She was helping him out of the shirt that had been specially designed to help support his weak arm.

"Of course not. I've been swimming since April Fool's Day, haven't I, Father?" He was wriggling out of his jeans as he spoke and now stood ready in scarlet underpants. "Wish me luck." He reached up to kiss first Julia, then Breckon. "You'll wait here?"

"Yes. And you'll give us a call when you're safe under the gate. And—"

"Be careful," interrupted Dominic. He gave them a mischievous grin and dived, shallow and smooth, into the water. The few strokes that took him down to the water gate showed Julia that he was indeed a strong swimmer in an extraordinary, triangular way. Now, for a moment, he trod water, waved his good hand at them, smiled that brilliant smile of his, and duck-dived neatly under the gate.

It was very quiet on the island. They were holding hands, watching ripples spread where the child had been. "Should we have let him?" asked Breckon.

"Yes. Whatever happens, it's better. You don't know your cousin Tarn. He's going to enjoy this." Her hand clenched in his. "Listen!"

"Hello," came the child's cry from the far side of the gate. "Can you hear me? I'm holding onto the gate, but I can't reach the bolt. The island looks quite near. I think I'll start now. Wish me luck."

And, "Good luck, Dominic," they called in unison, then turned to stare at each other strangely, still handfast, and then, at last, after all the years, to kiss.

Eleven

"NO!" Breckon lifted his head from hers. "We can't. Not while he's——"

"I know. Breckon, what can we do? Something, please or I think I'll go mad."

It earned her a reluctant laugh. "Not you too, love. I'm counting on you for the sanity of my family. Our family," he corrected himself. "And be damned to Uncle Paul and his 'taint.' "

"When you meet Cousin Tarn," said Julia sombrely,

"you may find yourself believing in that taint all over again."

"Maybe I will. But you're not Matron Andrews, thank God. And, besides, look at Dominic. The world can't have too many like him. We've got to save him, Julia."

"It rather looks as if he has to save us."

"I wish I knew how far it really is to that island."

"And what he'll find there. Breckon, do you think there is anything here we could use as a weapon? Just in case."

"It will be something to do," said Breckon. Which just about summed it up.

It was a rather random search, since one of them stayed, all the time close to the water gate. But, taking it in turns, they finally equipped themselves with a one-tined pitchfork, found by Julia under the straw in the shed, and a rusty but solid iron bar, which Breckon unearthed near the now well-trodden path up the hill. "There's something queer about that hill," he told her, returning with the bar. "I don't like this island a bit."

She could not help laughing, just out of the happiness of being with him again. "It's a funny thing," she said, "but I don't either." And then, with a quick, anxious glance at her watch: "Breckon, it will be dark soon. Do you think he had time enough?"

"He was the only judge," said Breckon. "And if I know him, which I should"—his hand, pressing hers, took away the sting of it—"he was right. But—we've been fools, Julia. He may need light—to find his way back, if he can start the boat."

"If he's got there." But already she was working

beside him, gathering last year's deadwood into a high pile. "I hope you're a Boy Scout," she said at last. "Or at least carry matches." ·

He felt in his pockets. "Damn. They've taken my lighter. But Dominic always has matches. He's rather clever at lighting them. They'll be in the inside pocket of his windbreaker."

Handling the small garment, she felt the tears come at last, and let them. Dominic had saved his matches rather than use them against the dark he feared. She held them out to Breckon. "It should be visible from the Torcello boats. Someone may come to investigate."

"You never know your luck." He lit a handful of dried leaves. "Don't cry, love. Whatever happens, this will have been worth it."

"I'm not crying," she lied, and added an armful of wood to the swiftly crackling fire. "Or not so much about us. It's Dominic. It seems such a waste." Why were they both assuming the worst? She picked up the windbreaker again. "Talking of weapons"—she felt in the cluttered pocket—"I'd clean forgotten Dominic's penknife. It's a good one. He said so. He said you always give good presents. You'd better have it. Just in case. . . ."

"Thanks." He tucked it in the right-hand pocket of his corduroys. "I remember—it's got a switch-blade. He promised never to use it. And—at least it will have the element of surprise. I think the fire's going well enough now, don't you? We don't want to be extravagant with our fuel."

"No." It was beginning to get dark. "I wish to God we'd thought of it sooner."

"Stupid," he agreed. "But it would be supider still

to turn an ankle trying to collect wood in the dark. We may need to be mobile."

"Yes. I wish we knew how far that island was." She kept coming back to it, to Dominic.

"Try not to fret, love. He may be busy trying to get the boat started. He's driven mine often enough, but it might so easily be different. Something he couldn't handle. I chose mine specially . . . to suit him. But it still seemed worth the try."

"Better than this waiting."

"For him. Perhaps best if he *doesn't* make it back."

"Yes." He moved away as she spoke, prowling around the circumference of the fire's light in search of more wood. "Do be careful." She could hardly see him as he moved into the undergrowth at the far side of the fire.

"I am careful." They were both thinking of Dominic. Then, suddenly, "Good lord! Julia, come here."

She threw a handful of small wood on the fire to give an extra burst of light and hurried towards him.

"How did we miss it this afternoon?" He was holding what looked like a small tree. "I was looking for dead wood and it just came away. It's been cut and put back."

"To mask a path. How many matches have we, Breckon?"

"Almost a full box, God bless Dominic. Keep an eye on the fire, love. I'm going to see where this goes. Straight into the hill, by the look of it. Not far," he reassured her, lighting a match and moving slowly away into the darkness, which was made more absolute by the light of the fire. The match flared and went out and she heard him swear to himself, then "Yes, it's a tunnel!" he exclaimed. "With a door. I did wonder. . . . Back in a second."

Another match showed for a moment, then vanished. She was biting her nails again. They tasted of smoke. She picked up the tree that had concealed the path and saw that it was an evergreen of some kind. That was why they had failed to notice it when they searched the island that afternoon. She began systematically pulling off branches and feeding them to the fire, which crackled and flared up merrily. The tree must have been cut for some time. Once again, she felt the cold finger of terror as she thought how systematically they had been prepared for. Breckon had found a tunnel. Was it their grave?

"Just what I thought." His voice came reassuringly out of the darkness. "The whole hill's artificial." He was nearer now. "An ammunition dump from the first world war, I should think." He emerged into the firelight. "Totally overgrown, maybe forgotten even."

"I hope it's empty. I suppose you couldn't see. . . ."

"No. I didn't want to use too many matches. It felt huge in there."

"Breckon, do you think—"

"Probably. I just don't quite see how it's going to work. Because they've got to find our bodies or they can't inherit."

"Your body. Dominic and I don't count."

"You count to me, my darling." His arm was warm around her. "I wish I understood. I wish we could plan. . . ."

"We'll just have to play it by ear. At least, we're together. I almost wish we hadn't let Dominic—"

"Hush!"

She could hear it, too. The sound of a powerboat, driven fast. Coming towards the island? Now, for the first time, she regretted their fire, which made it impossible to see any other light.

"Coming here, I think," said Breckon. "There will be a moment, whoever it is, while they get the gate open. We must challenge them; find out. Here." He handed her the pitchfork. "If it's them, remember, they mean to kill us. In a way, we can't lose." He hefted the metal bar. "I'm going to start with this and keep Dominic's penknife as a last resort. Remember not to let yourself get silhouetted against the fire, love. It's part of our element of surprise. And, it may bring help."

"This may *be* help." Once again, she wondered why they were both so pessimistic, then remembered all the evidence of careful, expensive, long-term planning. They were right to expect the worst.

The boat's engine roared, then cut out. In the silence that followed, she could hear the fire crackling, and then a thud as the boat hit the water gate. "Hello," said Dominic's cheerful voice. "Here we are."

"We?" Breckon took Julia's hand to lead her away from the fire and take up position on the decrepit landing stage.

"Yes. I got help." And then, in Italian, "Can you manage, Lucia?"

"The bolt is very stiff. There! There it comes."

Breckon's hand on Julia's was hard. "Lucia Capella," he whispered. "What in the name of—" The firelight showed the water gate slowly opening. "For God's sake, be careful."

"I am careful," whispered Julia. And then, loud and cheerful: "Dominic, darling, you made it!"

"Sure I did." The boat was nosing its way slowly up the channel to the landing stage. "And, see, I got help. They'd marooned poor Lucia on that island. She couldn't manage the boat," he explained, as it bumped the landing stage. "Well, nor could I, by myself. But together, here we are!"

"It's wonderful." There was an odd note in Breckon's voice. "Here! Out you come. Get your clothes on quick, Dom, you must be frozen. And let's get away from here." He made the mooring rope fast to the dock and held out a hand to Lucia. "Come and get warm by our fire while you wait."

"I may as well stay in the boat." Her English was fluent, though heavily accented.

"No." He reached down a firm hand and pulled her ashore. "Come and tell us how you got to be left on that island. I thought you'd gone home."

"I did." The girl held out shaking hands to the fire, her face pale in its light. "I got a message. A note." She spoke slowly, as if having trouble with her English. "About Dominic. It said he needed me. To tell no one, but take the train in to Venice. I'd be picked up at the bridge by the station."

"You didn't tell the police?"

"It said not to. That they'd . . . hurt Dominic. So I went."

"That was very brave of you," said Breckon. "What happened?"

"A water taxi picked me up. When we were well out in the lagoon, something happened; I don't know. I woke up and found myself alone on that island."

"Very odd indeed," said Breckon. "Are you two ready, Julia?"

"Yes." Dominic, rigid with cold, had done his best to help her get him into his clothes, but it had been a struggle, just the same, in the now dwindling light of the fire.

"Then let's go. Julia, I think you'd better sit in the back with Lucia." Standing between the two women, he quietly passed her the penknife. "Dominic and I will drive." He helped Julia and Lucia on board. Then, "Can I have the key, Dominic?"

"The key?" A shiver ran through Dominic's words. "But I left it in the lock."

"It's not there now." His voice hardened. "Hand it over, Lucia."

"But I haven't got it." Horribly, her voice carried conviction.

"What did you do with it? Hush, Dominic, it wasn't your fault. What did you do with it, Lucia?"

"Nothing. Perhaps I knocked it as I got out. Have you looked on the floor?"

"Of course I have." And then, head up, listening. "Too late anyway. Here they come. On shore, quick. We're sitting ducks here. Round to the back of the fire. Julia, you look after Lucia. Dom, give me a hand with the boat. I want to shove her off so she blocks the passage." And then, in quite a different tone. "Don't, Dom. You did splendidly. How were you to know she was one of them?"

"I should have." His voice was a child's now, desolate, but he worked with a will to help his father push the boat off from the landing stage.

"Don't." Julia slipped the penknife into the side-seam pocket of her skirt and caught Lucia's arm as she saw her move to intervene. How much of the judo training Sir Charles had made her take did she remember? "I hope I don't kill you," she said between her teeth, twisted, threw, and had the amazed Lucia's arms locked behind her. "Dominic!" She saw that the boat was well out in the channel by now, with Breckon using the one-tined pitchfork to guide it towards the water gate. "Come and give me a hand, would you? I need something to tie her up with."

"What?" Dominic's voice was still trembling with the shock of Lucia's treachery.

"The bits of my skirt. Do you remember? I brought them over, earlier, before we lit the fire. They're this side of it somewhere."

"I said they'd come in handy." It did Dominic good to be doing something. "Mother, what a fool . . . I never thought—"

"Don't, darling. We've all been fools—all the way, it seems to me. Thanks!" She took the scraps of material from him and knotted them tight around Lucia's slim wrists.

"You're wasting your time." Lucia, speaking coarse, peasant Italian, sounded a different creature. "He's too many for you all the way. Do you think you have a chance now? If you hurt me, he'll kill you."

"Oh?" Breckon had got the boat where he wanted it and came over to join them, his face dimly illuminated by the fire. "It's like that, is it?" The sound of the approaching boat was louder now, but he took no notice. "Tell me, Lucia, if I'd taken you to bed when you offered, would you be on my side now?"

"Never!" She spat at him. "He's worth a hundred of you. He's . . . he's a king."

"And here he comes. Hang on to her, Julia, while I put some more wood on the fire—and do exactly what I tell you. Exactly, understand. Dominic, here by me, and the same goes for you. I've got to be boss."

"Of course you have," said Dominic.

"Do you want me to gag her?" asked Julia.

"I don't think so. We may need her voice. Listen!" The sound of the approaching engine had dwindled. The driver must have seen that the water gate was open. "No lights," said Breckon. "Your friends are cautious, Lucia."

"Not friends," she said. "Friend. The others don't count."

"So friendly that he left you helpless on the island next door." And then, leaving it to sink in, "Here they come. Quiet!" The lightless boat was nosing its way very cautiously through the open gate. The fire had blazed up enough so that they could see three people on board. Four of them and three of us, thought Julia. But they would be armed. She tightened her grip on Lucia's helpless hands, and, for good measure, put her other hand over her mouth. No gag, but no words, yet.

"Lucia!" Tarn's voice, raised in fury. He must have seen the boat that lay between him and the dock. "What's going on here? Why the hell did you come over?"

Lucia bit Julia's hand, and got a savage twist at her own for her pains. Nobody spoke. Tarn and his companions were working in angry silence, pushing the loose boat out of the way and finally edging in to the dock. "Anyone moves, I'll shoot." Tarn jumped ashore first. His voice, edgy with uncertainty, told Julia that Breckon had been right in not launching an attack at once. Tarn's elaborate plans had gone badly wrong. He would not like that—and might miscalculate. "Lucia," he said again, "where the hell are you? What is all this?"

Both Julia and Dominic turned to look at Breckon, camouflaged like them from the arriving party by the dark bushes behind and the light of the fire in front. He put his finger on his lips. Lucia bit Julia's hand again, drew blood, and managed a kind of grunt in the process.

"There's someone there all right," said Tarn. "Behind the fire. Spread out. They can't be armed. Flashlights."

"Just a moment." Breckon spoke at last. "Cousin Tarn, I take it. You know my voice?"

"I should say so! But how the hell?" He turned angrily to one of his companions. "I thought you said you'd knocked him out for keeps."

"I was sure I had." A woman's voice. One of the Miss Browns?

"I've got a hard head," said Breckon. "So—I can make you an offer, Cousin. We've a hostage here, your girlfriend, Lucia. Let us go, and she goes free. Attack us, and we kill her."

"What with?" Tarn's voice intended scorn but showed a trace of doubt.

"A knife. Show her, Julia, and let her speak."

Could he mean it? But, even as a bluff, it was worth trying. Or—was it? Julia had a horrible feeling she

knew Tarn too well. Better than Breckon did. But she
had promised to obey him implicitly. Holding Lucia's
hands ruthlessly in her left one, she used her right to
press the catch of the switch-blade and shove its sharp
point, hard, under Lucia's left ribs.

Her mouth free, Lucia screamed. "Tarn! They're
killing me! They mean it."

"Good riddance," said Tarn. "Saves me a chore,
doesn't it? Told you to stay on the island, didn't I?"

"But the little bastard was starting the boat! I
thought——"

"I didn't hire you to think. Get on with it, Cousin,
she's all yours."

Lucia swore in gutter Italian. And then, "Dear God,
what have I done?"

"Been fooled like the rest of us," said Breckon.
"Let her go, Julia. She's on our side now, aren't you
Lucia?" He raised his voice as the three flashlight
bearers began a slow encircling movement round the
fire. "Very well, Cousin, since we know where we
stand, here's another offer for you. Half shares. I'd
have done it anyway, if I'd only known you existed."

"Thanks! I'll have it all, and no questions asked."
He and his companions were level with the fire now,
and Julia, looking up from untying Lucia's hands,
decided that the other two were indeed the Miss Browns,
looking surprisingly young and tough in jeans. But still
it shifted the odds ever so little. Specially with Dominic
as the unknown factor. "It's all a bloody bore." Tarn
stopped beside the fire, which cast strange lights on his
handsome, furious face. How had she ever thought it
like Breckon's? "I don't want to shoot you, Cousin,"

he went on now. "It wouldn't suit my plans at all. Maybe you're right. Fifty-fifty it is. Come out of those bushes and shake hands on it."

"Just a moment. We'll have to talk terms a little." From Breckon's voice, he had, in fact, moved farther into the bushes and, as Julia realised this, Dominic crept up beside her and caught her hand. "Father says, into the tunnel," he whispered. "Hands and knees. This way."

It made horrible sense. In a narrow tunnel, a metal bar was as powerful a weapon as a gun. Falling to her hands and knees, and noticing that Lucia did the same without comment, she heard Breckon talking steadily on, listing his proposals for a division of the estate. It sounded so convincing that for a horrible moment she wondered if he could be mad enough to mean it, and paused in her tracks, but an impatient twitch from Dominic in front made her hurry on. They were at the gap in the bushes now. "That way." Whispering, Dominic let go her hand and drew a little aside. "Father says I'm to come last. You know the way. Just keep to the path."

Here among the bushes it was possible to rise to an awkward stoop, and the path, too, was surprisingly well beaten. They soon reached what Julia's hands told her was a brick-arched opening in the hillside. "This way." She pulled Lucia after her into the tunnel entrance. Her questing hands found hinges at one side, and what must be an open door. No time to think of being shut in here. Breckon's orders. The tunnel was narrow, but high, and she felt her way along until a sudden feeling of space told her they had reached the main chamber, which was remarkably airy, if you discounted the smell of bats.

"I don't like it," whispered Lucia, gripping Julia's hand. "He'll kill us all. He's bound to."

"I do hope not." Julia managed to sound more cheerful than she felt. "Dominic—"

Silence answered her. And then, "Didn't you notice? He didn't come," said Lucia.

"Oh, my God!" Dominic was out there in danger, while she huddled here in comparative safety. On his own initiative, or on Breckon's orders? No way of telling, and nothing to do, herself, but go on obeying orders. A sound at the mouth of the tunnel sent her swiftly beside its entrance, switchblade in hand. But it was Breckon's voice that came, an unmistakable thread of whisper, out of the darkness. "Hang on, love. Don't clobber me."

"Breckon!" It was a breathless sigh of relief. "Thank God. But where's Dominic?"

"Having a go at starting their boat, while they're busy with us. You never know your luck. I bet Cousin Tarn has something very fancy in the automatic line. Just Dom's cup of tea."

"But he'll have taken the key from the ignition."

"Probably. But with time, and a hairpin, Dom or I could cope with that. So—we're going to play for time."

"A hairpin?"

"Dom always carries a hairpin. Just in case."

It was true. She remembered, now, that magpie collection in the windbreaker pocket. "Oh, Breckon, if *he* just gets away. . . ."

"If he gets way," said Breckon, "we three are safe. He'd make a damned good witness, our Dominic."

"Yes." The tears were dangerously near again at that use of the word "our." "Breckon, if we get out of here. . . ."

He reached out in the dark and found her hand. "When we get out of here," he said, "we're getting married—quick, before anything else happens."

There was a soft laugh from the far end of the tunnel. "Think of that," said Tarn Menzies. "They still don't know. Couple of babes in the woods, aren't you! God—of all the untidy—If it hadn't been for that, I reckon I'd have waited. But—nothing to wait for. Fine divorce you two got. In London. Right? Wife in England: English. Nobody thought to tell you an Englishwoman's domicile's her husband's. Doesn't matter where *she* is. Husband in Italy, she's in Italy, for all legal purposes. Ditto U.S. Were you still there, Cousin Breckon? Damned if I remember. Doesn't matter. Either way, no domicile, no divorce. I don't think you can have got the best lawyers, Cousin Julia. Thought you American, I suppose. Caught the accent. Funny, really. It's going to be the death of you, though. You're no more divorced than your dear Queen. And your little bastard, Dominic, is true blue legitimate."

"Well, I'll be damned," said Breckon.

"Yes, and very soon," breathed the voice from the other end of the tunnel. "Walked straight into my trap, didn't you? Of course, it's going to take a bit of explaining, darling Julia being in there, too. Maybe, with luck, there will be enough bits of her left around so we can dump them outside. Trying to run away . . . too short a fuse . . . just like a woman. Well, we'll see. Any last words before I light the fuse?"

"Fuse?" Breckon's voice sounded high with shock. "What do you mean?"

"I mean you've gone to ground in a world war ammunition dump, and, funny thing, by some accident, enough ammo got left in there to blow up a regiment. Or, at least, it's there now. The police will have to decide, won't they, whether darling Julia did it on purpose, for revenge, which would be like her, or by accident, like a fool, which would be more like her still. Either way, we'll be miles away." He laughed. "We are right now, the Miss Browns and I, back in my bedroom at the hotel, playing poker with a couple of friends. Anything else to say, Cousin, before I set light to the slow match and blow you all to hell?"

"Yes." Breckon sounded desperate now. "I'll give you three-quarters."

"Fancy that." Mockingly—"Generous, ain't you? But, thanks just the same, I think I'll have it all."

"Tarn!" Lucia suddenly spoke up, from her position across the tunnel entrance from Julia and Breckon. "You don't understand. Dominic's not here."

"God, I could kill you," said Breckon.

And, "Thanks, love. That settles it," said Tarn. "Here goes the match to your slow fuse. Don't worry, any of you. We'll round up young Dominic in time to arrange an accident for him, too."

They heard the sputter as he lit a match, then: "Come on, Meg, Fran. Leave them to fry while we find the kid. He'll be at the boat, natch. Good-bye, Julia darling, Lucia love." A slam was the shutting of the door. Then, his voice muffled through it. "Damnation. Where's the padlock?"

"In my pocket!" shouted Breckon. "Come and get it, Cousin."

Julia had been straining her ears for any sound of a boat starting, but now the silence was absolute, except for a frantic scrabbling at the other side of the door, where she could hear Tarn exhorting the Miss Browns to find him something—anything—that he could use to wedge the hasp. "They're bound to find something," she whispered, hanging on to Breckon's hand as if for dear life—or, she thought, dear death.

"Yes. But it will take time. Give Dom a chance. As for you—" In the stifling darkness, Julia felt him let go of her clinging hand. She heard a scuffle, the sound of a blow, and then a soft thud. "That will keep her out of mischief for a while," said Breckon, regaining possession of Julia's hand. "A traitor, right now, is what we can do without."

"Breckon, how long do you think?"

"Shh . . ." Gently, firmly, as if for all time, he pulled her to him and kissed her. Then, just as she was beginning to forget everything, even death, even Dominic, in the magic of it, he let her go. "Hush, my love," he said again. "Quiet, and don't fret. I'm off to see how they're getting on with the door."

"But, Breckon! Shouldn't we be looking for the fuse?"

"Sweet idiot." His voice was only a thread of sound, close to her ear. "You've forgotten—what they don't know—that I've got matches. I cut it the first time I came down. When I took the padlock."

"I'm a fool."

"I love you. Keep an eye on Miss Double-Cross there. I want to keep them occupied right here as long as they dare stay. That's what we don't know."

Alone with the knowledge that she was not, at least, going to die in the next few moments, Julia felt her way over to where Lucia lay in a heap, breathing stertorously. Not much she could do for her in this solid darkness. Not much she could do for herself. Her legs suddenly gave way underneath her, and she sat down, heavily, on the ground beside Lucia.

Breckon had reached the end of the tunnel. She heard him lunge against the door, and a soft laugh from Tarn outside. "Want out, do you? Too bad." The door must have a grating of some kind in it, she thought. For ventilation, no doubt. It was a comforting thought. They might not be going to be blown to pieces, but they were still prisoners. Would one rather die of suffocation, or of hunger and thirst?

Still no sound of a boat. What had happened to Dominic? She would not let herself think about him. But how could she stop? Suddenly, there was a confusion of voices from outside. Both Miss Browns were talking at once. Tarn was answering, quickly, angrily. Impossible to make out what was going on. Now, Tarn was giving orders, sharp, furious.

"Julia?" Breckon was back, finding her hand in the blackness.

"Yes." Like him, she kept her voice to a shadow of a whisper.

"They missed Dom at the boat. He got away. But not in her; he hadn't got her started. God knows where he is. But at least they haven't got him. They're panicking now. They think this hill's going up any moment. They've got the door wedged tight, I'm afraid. They're spreading out to look for Dom. They won't find him. Not if I know Dom."

"Not in the dark." They both knew that, come daylight, he would not stand a chance on this small island with its dearth of cover. "How long do you think it will be before they begin to realise?"

"That this isn't going up? Hard to tell. It's unpredictable stuff, I believe, slow match. And goodness knows what kind of an expert Cousin Tarn is. One thing—I bet they'll play safe. After all, they've got all night."

"Unless the fire brings someone. They must have thought of that."

"Yes. They're bound to have doused it, but it's helping panic them, thank God. That, and not being able to find Dom."

And, as if in answer, Tarn's voice from outside: "Can you hear me, Cousin Breckon?"

"Yes." Breckon moved cautiously forward, a little way down the tunnel, and Julia followed him.

"We've got the kid. Little one-hand in person. Say hello to your father, Cousin Dominic. You don't want to? Then we'll have to make you, won't we?"

"Hush." Breckon's hand was steadying on Julia's. They could both hear what sounded like a scuffle outside, then a voice said, "Hello, Father."

"I don't believe it," said Breckon.

"Want me to start handing in his fingers through the grating? He can't spare them all that well, can you, tiny Cousin?"

"I still don't believe it."

He was answered by a sudden, horrible scream.

"Shh." Breckon's hand on hers was all that stood between Julia and madness. "That's not Dom," he whispered to her. "I promise you. Trust me, Julia?"

"Yes." She must.

"OK." He raised his voice. "You've got us. You've got him. What next?"

"You come out of there—the three of you. Hands in air, dead still when you're out." He laughed, the laugh that Julia had once found so attractive. "Dead's the word. Tiresome about our little fireworks display. Something seems to have gone wrong with the fuse."

"Something did."

"Goddamn you." Tarn's voice rose and cracked. "Think you're clever, don't you? You, who've danced on my string all these years. Christ, I'm going to show you. Doesn't matter if you're marked up. Or the kid. And darling Julia can watch. More fun this way, really. Right, out you come. You first, Cousin. Darling Julia next. And lovely Lucia last."

"There's one difficulty about that," said Breckon. "Lucia's unconscious."

"Unconscious? How?" His voice rose another note.

"Because I knocked her out." Breckon kept his tone casual. "She seemed a bit confused about whose side she was on. Well, I can't altogether blame her. If I were the Miss Browns, I know I'd be thinking pretty hard by now. Such a clever plan, wasn't it, Cousin, and not one bit of it going right." He was deliberately goading Tarn, Julia realised, as well as playing for time. If only she was sure that Tarn had not got Dominic. But at least they were no longer—if they had been—torturing him. Stupid. Breckon did not believe they had him. Breckon knew his voice infinitely better than she did. She must assume that Breckon knew best.

Twelve

BRECKON was kissing her, hard, as if it must last forever. "I don't know if we're going to get out of this," he whispered. "But whatever happens, Julia, I love you. Always have, always will."

"And I you."

"It's more than I deserve. God, what a fool I was, back at La Rivière."

"You couldn't know."

"No. Who would believe in a monster like Cousin Tarn? And—I loved Uncle Paul. No excuse, though."

"Stop whispering and come out of there." Tarn's voice, on a still higher note, from outside. "Unless you want to hear the kid squeal again. It'll be a bit of him, this time."

Julia felt Breckon go rigid and knew, horribly, that he was not, in fact, sure whether they had Dominic or not. "We're coming. Only, we've lost the tunnel entrance. Can you feel it, Julia?"

"No." They were standing beside it.

"Well, find it, and quick. You've got matches, haven't you?"

"I finished them." Breckon's voice was deceptively meek. "You feel that way and I'll feel this, Julia. It has to be somewhere near." They stood stock-still, handfast, in the darkness. "For God's sake watch out for Cousin Tarn's little bomb." He moved noisily away from the tunnel entrance, pulling Julia with him.

Outside, a Miss Brown said something. "Sure," came Tarn's voice. "Good idea. Open it up and flash a light down. There's your exit, you two. Out you come. Julia first. Hands up and no nonsense or the kid's had it."

"Coming." Breckon pressed Julia's hand. "I can see it now. We'd got half across the cave. Careful, Julia, watch out!" He scuffled his feet loudly and whispered: "I think he's losing control. He might do anything. We've got to go out fighting. One of them will be out of sight, pretending to hold Dom. Which makes it even. And, remember, they don't want to shoot us. It's our best chance."

"Yes." They both knew it for a slim one.

A furious shout from Tarn blended with a screech. Dominic? A Miss Brown? Julia could not tell. Nor, she now feared, could Breckon. "Coming!" The flashlight, shining straight in at the mouth of the tunnel, half-blinded her after the darkness. She took the tunnel as fast as she dared, remembering something. Both Miss Browns were left-handed. She had noticed it the very first time they had met, on the train at Victoria, but never consciously remembered it until now. So—the left hand holding the flashlight. A Miss Brown facing the tunnel, standing, inevitably, to the left as she emerged. She was out, dodging, swinging leftwards, missing, by inches, the blow that should have stunned her, and then grappling, silently, horribly, in the darkness with an opponent stronger than herself. Noise close by suggested that Breckon was also out of the tunnel, and fighting. No shot, thank God. No light. The flashlight must have dropped and broken, the fire must be nearly out. Whichever Miss Brown she was fighting had muscles of iron and knew her judo, too. And, inevitably, her left-handedness gave her an advantage.

Now, nearby, Tarn's voice rose in a breathless torrent of obscenities, describing, in detail, what he was going to do to Breckon, Dominic, and her. Her attention distracted for a moment, Julia gave her opponent an opening and found herself lying helpless on the ground, Miss Brown, triumphant, on top of her. "Hang on, my darling." Miss Brown's voice throbbed with pleasure. "I'll just knock this one out and be with you." She half-throttled Julia with one hand and felt about her with the other, presumably for the flashlight.

"Don't." The voice of the younger Miss Brown. "Don't, Meg. Listen!"

Tarn choked to silence on a four-letter word, and

they all heard the roar of a fast-approaching boat. Julia, wriggling a little in Miss Brown's grasp, turned her head far enough to see light approaching from the direction of the water gate. Help. But for whom?

The engine cut out. Close by, she thought that Breckon and Tarn had stopped fighting to listen. Then into the sudden silence, came Dominic's voice. "Mother? Father? Are you all right? It's real help this time."

"Sure is." A man's voice. Familiar. Of course—Peter and Susan. "Armed to the teeth, in case anyone cares. Been looking all over for you, ma'am. Are you OK?"

The grip on Julia's throat slackened. A voice, almost unrecognisable, but Tarn's, whispered, "Quick, this way."

"Coming, my darling." Miss Brown was gone.

Stiffly, shakily, Julia sat up. "Here, Dom," she called. "We're all right. I think." And then, her voice rising. "Breckon?" No answer. "Breckon!"

A flashlight shone on her. The girl, Susan, bent over her. "Are you hurt, Mrs. Rivers?"

"I don't think so. But, Breckon. . . ." Peter, also with flashlight in hand, was bending over something that lay very still on the ground. Dominic was there too, an odd figure apparently wrapped in somebody's jacket.

"It's all right, ma'am." Peter's voice was extraordinarily reassuring. "He's just knocked out. Flashlight and gun, Sue, while I take a good look."

"Do be careful." Julia got dizzily to her feet. "He'd been knocked out once already."

"I did it as gently as I dared," came the younger Miss Brown's voice from the darkness. "Please. I want to give myself up. I had no idea . . . he's off his head, I think."

"So do I," said Julia.

"Very well." Peter rose and faced in the direction her voice had come from, torch in left hand, gun in right. "Come out slowly, hands up." And, as she emerged, cautiously, into the circle of light: "Where are the others?"

"In the cave. My sister went with him. I pretended I was coming. We ought to get away." She looked nervously over her shoulder in the direction of the tunnel. "He's capable of anything when he's like this. And—there's enough explosive in there to pretty well blow up the island."

"Right," said Peter. "Flashlight for you, Dominic. Flash and gun for you, ma'am. Shoot her if she does anything out of line. Sue and I will carry Mr. Rivers."

"No need." Breckon sat up shakily. "She's right. His mind's been cracking since his plans started fouling up. We'd better get the hell out of here. Give me a hand up, Dom. What on earth have you got on?"

"Talk later." Peter turned to lead the way. "Come on." His boat lay alongside Tarn's, and it was awkward, desperate work getting across and into it by torchlight. "Watch Miss Brown, Sue." Peter was busy with the rope that moored the boat to Tarn's.

"I've got a gun in her ribs," came Sue's reassuring voice, from the cabin.

"There's no need," wailed Miss Brown. "Honestly, I've been doing my best for you ever since he sent the rest of the gang away. Only my sister, Meg, kept such a close eye on me, I couldn't do much. But I only gave you half the injection, Mrs. Rivers, and I didn't hit

Breckon nearly so hard as I could have. I hope you don't mind my calling you Breckon," she added, absurdly. "I feel I know you so well."

"I should just about think you did." Breckon caught the rope Peter threw on board and moved over to make room for him in the driver's seat. "I hope she's fast, this boat of yours."

"Fastest in Venice. That's why we hired her. And just as well." The engine roared into life: Peter switched on the headlights and took the water gate full tilt.

"She's faster than yours, Father," said Dominic, as the engine settled down to a steady, expensive purr.

"Lucky for us. But I don't understand——"

And, simultaneously, "Dom, you're wet!" exclaimed Julia.

"Well, of course he's wet." Peter turned around to tell her. "Where d'you think we found him? We'd lost track of you, see, after you vanished from the Da Rimini. So'd the police." He laughed. "They were running around in circles, but we knew something they didn't. We knew about Tarn Menzies. So——when we found both his boats gone, we put up a prayer and came out here to look around the lagoon. Needle in a haystack, if you like. Only time he'd ever been out here that we knew of was when he took you to Torcello, ma'am. Not much clue there. And all these damned islands. So there we were, cruising down the Torcello channel, keeping our eyes open, and what do we see but friend Dominic sitting on one of those channel lights, waving and shouting. So, natch, we picked him off, and here we are. Or, rather, there we were." He slowed the engine to run quietly. "Far enough now. I reckon we ought to wait and see."

"It's horrible." Julia kept thinking of Lucia back there in the cave, helpless. "But, Dom, you mean you swam to the channel? In your clothes?" She could feel his soaking jeans against her leg.

"Well, I had to," Dominic explained. "The other Miss Brown caught me at the boat before I'd even got out my hairpin, so I went over the side, and out the water gate, quick. I got out of my jacket, all right, but jeans. . . . Actually, I was glad of them when it came to climbing up that post. It was covered with mussels. Very scratchy."

"Damned lucky, that was all," said Peter soberly. "Some of them are live, I think." He stopped. "He's quite something, this son of yours, Mrs. Rivers."

"Ours." Breckon reached back to feel for Julia's hand. "I guess that's twice you've saved our lives, Dom."

"But poor Lucia!" Julia could not forget her. "She's in the cave."

"She sold out, didn't she?" said their Miss Brown. "Trouble with that Tarn was, he was too attractive. He never bothered with me. He knew I'd always do what Meg said. Well, almost always. Oh, my God!" The shattering roar of the explosion drowned her voice. The centre of the island had blown out and a tongue of livid flame illuminated their drawn faces as they sat there, silenced by the force of the blast, gazing first at the island, where now trees and buildings were burning fiercely, then at each other with a kind of questioning horror.

The noise that had hurt their ears was succeeded by a series of lesser rumblings, and the crackling of fire.

"Dominic, don't look!" Julia's arm was close around him, and she felt him tremble.

"I . . . I must." For the first time, she heard the catch of tears in his voice. "There's Lucia. Poor Lucia. She . . . she was good to me. I'm sure she didn't mean . . ." He voiced the question that was in all their minds. "Is there any chance?"

"I'm afraid not." Peter's voice was grim, but he made it calm. "Not a hope in hell; and not a thing we can do that the police can't do better. And a lot simpler if they don't find us here." The boat was tossing now as the shock waves from the explosion reached it, and a smoking bit of rock splashed into the water nearby. "I think we'd best make tracks. Get out of here and find young Dominic some dry clothes." He revved the engine. "Don't cry, Miss Brown. Just thank God you weren't there."

"Tarn meant me to be." She was crying, but quietly. "I couldn't make Meg see that he didn't mean to leave any loose ends."

"No," said Peter thoughtfully, "you're right. No loose ends. It will suit Sir Charles down to the ground, come to think. I wonder . . ."

"Sir Charles?" asked Julia, but Miss Brown's voice drowned hers. "He sent the others away." She swallowed a sob. "Tarn. Yesterday—after it was all set up for tonight. He was mad as hell because they roughed him up so, night before last, when he staged the 'attack' on the two of you, Mrs. Rivers." She laughed, surprisingly, hiccupping through her tears. "I rather think they enjoyed it—hurting him, making him swear. He paid them off in the morning. They're safe back where they belong now. It made me wonder what kind of plans he had for Meg and me." She was crying quietly again. "Poor Meg, she loved him so."

"He could be very attractive," said Julia. "When he wanted to. But, Peter," she tried again. "What did you mean about Sir Charles?"

"He wouldn't much want loose ends either," said Peter.

"But I don't understand," began Julia, and once more had to give way to Miss Brown's passionate monologue.

"Meg just wouldn't see. I tried to make her after what happened to that girl Pamela at Victoria. She wouldn't face it. She thought the sun rose and set in Tarn. It was just an accident, she insisted. But I'm sure Tarn held on to her—Pamela, I mean. I saw her face, back there on the platform. And then we read about it in the papers. She was badly hurt. I kept on telling Meg it was too dangerous. But, you see, we needed the money so badly." She turned to stare back at the flaming island, now safely behind them. "No pensions. Nothing. Meg invested our savings on Aunt Andrews' advice. They were going to double themselves. They didn't, of course. We were at our wits' end when Cousin Tarn turned up with his story and his offer. Meg thought it was terribly romantic. You know: the missing heir, and all that? Well, so did I. At first. It all seemed so simple. A little help, of a perfectly legal kind, he said, to sort things out and prove his claim, and he'd be rich, and make us independent for life. All he asked, to begin with, was that we talk to you on the train and make sure you shared his carriage. If it didn't happen naturally."

"Which it did. God help me!" Julia spoke almost

automatically, her mind still working on those strange references to Sir Charles.

"Yes. You can see, it all seemed harmless enough. By the time we began to understand what kind of 'help' Tarn really meant, we were too deep in, or so Meg thought. He could make her believe anything. That's why he kept us on when he sent the others away. His father, Paul Rivers, had hired them, see. He thought he could do better, plan better than Paul."

"He was off his head," said Breckon.

"At the end, I'm sure. He hated you so. I think, really, he hated everyone. I just wonder how long it would have been before he turned on his father. He refused to be called Rivers, you know, or Antony. I thought, all the time, his making us call him Tarn was queer. As if he wanted no part of the family. I don't like to think what would have happened to them . . ." And then, "What are you going to do with me?"

"It's a good question." Peter slowed the boat. "What do you think, Mr. Rivers?"

"We need evidence." Breckon was considering it. "Against Paul Rivers and Miss Andrews—his wife. Miss Brown's right, I'm sure. Paul planned this. All of it. As he did, before, back at La Rivière. It only went wrong this time when Tarn took over, thought he knew best."

"Right," said Peter. Ahead of them somewhere a siren screamed and he turned quickly to make sure that they were far enough away from the glow that was the island.

"I'll give you the evidence," Miss Brown said eagerly. "It's all at Tarn's hotel. Paul told him to burn his instructions, but he kept them just the same. 'Just in case,' he said. It did make me wonder about him. About it all."

"As well you might." Peter was looking ahead now, to where the lights silhouetted Venice against the sky. "Let's go, then, and get them—the instructions. Dominic's tough, bless him. He'll stand another half hour, won't you, Dom?"

"Course I will."

But, "There's no need," Breckon argued. "In fact, better not. Let the police find the papers."

"If we trust Miss Brown?" Peter made it a question.

"I don't see why not." Breckon's voice was kind. "She's got a lot to gain."

"You *can,*" wailed Miss Brown.

"You're not police?" Julia was shaken by a fear she did not want to recognise.

"Well." Peter did not like what he had to tell her. "Not exactly. Not here. You should know, Mrs. Rivers. Just say we're friends of Sir Charles'. Not very competent ones, I'm afraid. He'll tear a proper strip off us when he sees us." His voice changed. "*If* he sees us. What do you think, Sue?"

"Peter, I don't know." Sue's voice was unhappy. "I only know we have to tell Mrs. Rivers. All of it."

"That's right." The others were aware that the two of them were communicating on a very deep level. Clearly, thought Julia, through that vague, growing horror, there was nothing of pretense about their relationship. "We only got on to it when we started discussing the case," Peter went on. "We'd worked separately before. This time we were together."

"Sir Charles' mistake," said Sue.

"One of them." They were close to Murano now, coming in rather north of the main channel, as fire-fighting and ambulance boats screamed out along it towards the island. He stopped the boat. "Look, I think we ought to sort this out before we land. Once we do, it's the police, Sir Charles, the lot."

"Sir Charles?" This time it was Breckon who asked the question.

"Yes, Sir Charles," Sue said. "He's been sitting it out in Florence. Waiting. Couldn't keep away, I suppose. Dollars to doughnuts he's in Venice by now."

"Waiting?" Julia's voice shook. "What do you mean?" And, once again, was aware of a silent exchange between Peter and Sue.

"He'd put a lot of money into you." Peter's voice was apologetic.

"And a lot of affection," said Sue.

"Love, I think."

"I always wondered." This is a conversation they had had before.

"So—" Peter took it up. "You've got to understand, Mrs. Rivers. He didn't want to lose you. For all kinds of reasons. And—he's a powerful man. He's used to getting what he wants."

"What are you trying to say?" The full horror of it had hit Julia, now, and sounded in her voice. Breckon reached around to find her hand and hold it.

"He wanted you two to quarrel," said Peter. "Once and for all. That's why he kept out of touch. To let it all happen."

"Of course he didn't want you hurt," put in Sue. "So he sent us to keep an eye on you. Only, we began to wonder. You see, I was the assistant who 'got ill' years ago in New York."

"What?" This was Breckon.

"Yes. He sent me home. Suddenly. Without explanation. Well, you know Sir Charles. He doesn't explain."

"And sent for me," said Julia. "Calling it an emergency." Breckon had been jealous. Breckon had been right. Horrible.

"Well," said Peter, "when Sue told me that, I remembered a friend of mine telling me about hiring a lawyer for a divorce case. He felt guilty about it. The girl was a protégée of Sir Charles'. And the lawyer was no good, he said."

"Me?" said Julia. "But, why?"

"He didn't want you free, don't you see? Anything might have happened. With a divorce that wasn't a divorce, he had you where he wanted you. Any time. And then, most of all, he didn't want you to keep the child. If you did, he knew he was bound to lose you."

"Dominic." She felt sick. And then, taking it all in, reluctant, appalled. "You mean he knew—Sir Charles—all the time? Where Dominic was?"

"One does somehow assume so. I mean"—Peter sounded miserable—"he would, wouldn't he?"

"Dear God, what a fool I've been. And he let me come. . . ."

"With us to protect you. Not his fault we made such a muck of it. He wanted your enemies rounded up all right. That's what I meant about the explosion suiting him so well. He just didn't want to lose you in the process. To them—or to your husband. Difficult for him—"

"Difficult!"

"Never mind, Mother." Dominic's teeth were chattering. "It didn't work, after all."

"In the end." She thought of the empty years, when she had put all her lonely misery into working for Sir Charles. "It's unspeakable."

"Yes." Peter had come to terms with it. "Power's bad for people. That's why we're quitting, Sue and I. Don't laugh—we're going to Australia, where Tarn Menzies didn't come from, to raise cattle—and kids, I hope. In the meantime, your Dominic's freezing to death, and we've got to decide about Miss Brown. As I see it, right now, officially, she's ashes, out there on that island. If we dropped her at Murano, she could get a *vaporetto* to the station and be anywhere in Europe by tomorrow morning. Shall we vote on it?"

"But I wouldn't know what to do," wailed Miss Brown. "Meg always arranged everything. I want to go on being me."

"Very sensible," said Breckon. "Don't worry too much, Miss Brown. We'll do the best we can for you."

"State's evidence," agreed Peter. "Satisfactory. Right." The boat speeded up. "In that case, I'll drop you and Dominic first, Mr. Rivers, take Mrs. Rivers home to the Da Rimini, then go and make our peace with the police, hope to God we can dodge Sir Charles, and do the best we can for Miss Brown."

"Fine," said Breckon, and Julia's heart shrivelled. "Except—didn't you say Sir Charles would be in Venice by now?"

"Bound to be, I should think. At the Da Rimini, waiting to be thanked."

"And rewarded," suggested Sue.

"He takes enough for granted," said Breckon. "Do you want to see him, Julia?"

"Dear God, no. Never again, if I can help it."

"That's fine with Sue and me," said Peter cheerfully. "What he doesn't know won't hurt him. I'd just as soon not have his long arm reaching out to make mincemeat of us in Australia, eh, Sue?"

"I'll say."

"Right," said Breckon. "There we are then. Like it or not, love, you'd best come home with Dom and me. I'll deal with Sir Charles in the morning. Tactfully. 'No loose ends.'" There was a smile in his voice as he quoted Peter's phrase. "I'll enjoy that. And thank you two properly, too. For everything. Right now, we must get Dom here home to bed."

"Home," said Julia, beginning to believe it.

"Good," said Dominic.